Gideon McGee's Dream

by

William Marshall

Zacharaias Press
P.O. Box 163
86 Sunnyside St.
Yantic, CT 06389

Library of Congress
Cataloging-in-Publication Data

97-90165

Marshall, William
Gideon McGee's Dream

ISBN: 0-9657575-0-1

Cover design by David Joslin

Cover photo courtesy of NASA

Printed in the USA by

MORRIS PUBLISHING

3212 East Highway 30 • Kearney, NE 68847 • 1-800-650-7888

Tell me not in mournful numbers
  Life is but an empty dream!'-
For the soul is dead that slumbers,
And things are not what they seem.

Longfellow, A Psalm of Life

DEDICATION

Gideon McGee's Dream is dedicated to all of us who have traveled into the dark night of the soul and wondered, "Is this all there is?" It is dedicated to my daimon, whose insistent pull despite my resistance, has granted me the vision to see the hazy outline of what I am capable of becoming.

ACKNOWLEDGMENTS

My thanks go to all those who have read the early versions of *Gideon McGee's Dream* and provided their enthusiastic support for moving this project forward. In particular I'm grateful to the boys and men of my mentoring community, Boys to Men, Inc., whose feedback was invaluable in the development of the book. Special thanks go to Sharon Wildermann whose insight and artistry created the figure of Gideon McGee that appears on the four corners of the book's cover.

INTRODUCTION

Gideon McGee's Dream is the story of a fourteen-year-old's search for meaning in a world where consciousness is taught to be an epiphenomenon of matter, where miracles go unexplained, or explained away by science, and where Isaac Newton and Rene Descartes have been the Gods of choice for the past three-hundred years. Gideon McGee has grown up in a world seemingly without justice, where bad things happen to good people and good things happen to bad people. His is a world where coincidence is an accident, luck is a lady who bestows her gifts randomly, and evil is projected onto an external devil.

Gideon McGee is the adolescent in all of us who, at one time or another during our dark night of the soul, has cried out in despair, "What kind of God are you!" *Gideon McGee's Dream* is an attempt to bring meaning into a world that has lost its way and thinks it has lost its soul. Some of the worlds Gideon visits represent ancient tales from the Earth's wisdom traditions, while others are newly formed from my twentieth century imagination. Some of the worlds in the story may touch you. Others may not. Take what serves you and leave the rest behind. Maybe, like Parsifal in the Land of the Gatekeeper, you'll come back to it many years later.

Chapter One

Its home was twenty-four trillion miles distant in the spiral galaxy called the Milky Way, and the odds of it happening would have been ridiculously large had there been anyone on the planet to make the calculation. At twenty-five thousand miles per hour the collision destroyed both the asteroid and the moon that circled the smallest and outermost planet of the far away sun called Alpha Centauri A. It was the largest of a triple sun system.

Most of the debris remained in orbit around the undiscovered planet, but a Mexico-sized chunk broke free of the gravitational pull of the miniature orb. The rogue slab of celestial junk began its trek into the far reaches of space following the unconscious call of its neighboring star's third planet.

Gideon McGee awoke in a panic, his dream jarring the peace that usually accompanies sleep. His brother Simon, three years his senior at seventeen, remained blissfully asleep in the bunk overhead. It had been three weeks since Gideon last slept through the night. Fourteen years of dreamless sleep, or so he thought, and now this. Night after night of sleep-demolishing dreams curdled Gideon McGee's already-sour personality. The few friends he had were bailing out, avoiding him much like a fish avoids air.

Not all of Gideon McGee's dreams were sleep stealers. Some compensated him for the nightmares that drew dark circles under his chestnut brown eyes. One such dream was of four desert wanderers who had been in search of a fabled city of gold for

1

many years, as their brown and leatherlike skin bore witness. Their pilgrimage had been long and arduous, filled with many trials of body and spirit, as any adventure should be. One day, one of the group, while despairing of ever finding the city of gold, spied a magnificent walled castle on the horizon. Curious and excited they made their way to the towering outer wall.

The first wanderer scaled the summit, screamed out in ecstasy and jumped over. Two more wanderers followed the first. When the last wanderer reached the top of the wall and realized he had found the city of gold he turned and looked back upon the desert. There he saw other wanderers, lost and in despair, unable to see the city of gold although it should have been plainly visible. In this dream Gideon realized he was the fourth wanderer. He woke up, not knowing if he jumped into the city of gold alone, or climbed back down to show others the way. It was the memory of the city of gold that always escorted Gideon back to sleep after one of his nightmares.

Until he had his big dream, Gideon McGee, in manner and attitude, resembled a teenage Ebenezer Scrooge, always complaining, forever cynical. His smile, which occurred only on the rarest of occasions, revealed a mouth whose corners were unaccustomed to turning heavenwards, and if listened to carefully one could almost hear them creak at the effort when they did. His smiles seemed like accidents, no sooner released than reeled back in like a hooked fish.

Life to Gideon McGee was something to protect himself against, something he had no part in creating or controlling. Slights and insults, back stabbings done to him and by him; heartbreak, for which he was never responsible; luck, that always went against him, comprised the downside of life that Gideon

2

seemed to live in. The upside was reserved for Simon, who was bigger, stronger, smarter and better looking than Gideon. All of Simon's advantages, to Gideon's way of thinking, were the result of luck.

Although Simon's skills were difficult for Gideon to attain, it was not until his sister Prudences' arrival when he was four, that the struggle to turn the corners of his mouth up or down, was decided in favor of a frown. By the time he was fourteen his attitude about life was etched on his face. His brown eyes, that seemed wider apart and brighter at four were now closer to the bridge of his nose, and only sparkled when life played one of its tricks on someone else. To Gideon's mind he had no more control over the way things were than a feather bobbing in a turbulent sea had of controlling the tides.

* * *

The McGee family lived on the outskirts of a middle-sized New England town that in its heyday, a hundred years earlier, was the center of a booming textile industry. Today, however, it was like any other city struggling to meet the needs of its citizens. The McGee house, a brown three bedroom Cape, sat on three wooded acres and could be approached only by a poorly repaired, snake-like dirt road that shortened by half the life of the shock absorbers of the McGee car. In the summer months the McGee's Taurus kicked up so much dust on their road it resembled a winter fog, and the sweat on Gideon's face ran like rivulets of mud.

It was a colder time now, the first day of the New Year, and Gideon awoke to a clatter outside his window that sounded like the tapping of a thousand drumsticks on a pane of glass. Because of his fitful sleeping of late, Gideon McGee was usually difficult to awaken for he only found peace as the sun was about to make its appearance above the horizon. This morning, however, it took nothing more substantial than his curiosity.

As sleepy as he was from his night of unsettling dreams, he nevertheless threw off his covers, yawned like an Appalachian hound dog, rubbed the sleep from his eyes with his bony knuckles, then surveyed the dusky room.

He looked at his older brother on the upper bunk. "Hey, Simon. Are you asleep?" Gideon asked, in a voice soft enough not to wake his brother if he wasn't awake already.

Receiving no answer, which was the answer he expected, Gideon slid out of bed and walked to the window. The pupils of his eyes were still dilated from his sleep, and therefore exquisitely sensitive to sunlight. Neither his mind, nor his eyes were prepared for the sight that was about to register on his senses. Gideon's bedroom window faced west, so that the coat of ice from the storm the night before reflected the eastern rising sun's rays back into his eyes. When his vision recovered from what he at first thought was a bomb blast, Gideon beheld a light show that only nature could provide and no rock concert could match.

Every tree, every branch, every blade of grass and every rock had grown a crystal skin that sparkled with its own internal light. Like an electric spark, the sun danced from surface to surface leaving an afterimage on Gideon's eyes and bringing the hibernating woods back to life. Nature had connected the world outside his window by a cosmic web of light. The wind blew from the north causing the tree branches to tap out their song against each other much like small children playing patty cakes. Gideon stood transfixed as the light danced and skipped from surface to surface. His eyes and ears had never been so pleasantly bombarded, yet he could not identify the feeling it had created.

"Spectacular, isn't it, Gideon?" Simon asked, placing his

hand lightly on his brother's shoulder so as not to startle him.

Gideon didn't hear Simon get out of bed, for despite his large size he was as graceful as the wind that blew through the crystallized trees. Gideon jumped at the touch, as though responding to a horn blast he wasn't expecting. Simon removed his hand.

"Why'd you sneak up on me like that?" Gideon barked, more embarrassed that he was caught enjoying the view than being startled by his brother.

"Sorry. I thought you heard me get up," Simon said absently, captured by the view that had so recently entranced his younger brother.

"Well, I didn't," Gideon shot back, glaring into the hazel eyes of his brother that hovered six inches above his own.

Simon turned away from the window and looked at his brother. "Why have you been so hostile lately? You're normally a royal pain, but for the past few weeks you've kicked it up to a new level."

Gideon began to fidget with his fingers, making cricket sounds with his fingernails. "Do you ever dream?" he asked, almost apologetically.

"Sometimes. Why do you ask?" Simon said as he placed his hand back on his brother's shoulder. He redirected his attention to the newly created winter scene and forgot his younger brother's question. "Last night I almost got killed in this ice storm while driving home from Maureen's."

"Yeah, so what?" Gideon said, almost wishing Simon had, and then feeling guilty at the thought.

Simon looked at Gideon with narrowed eyes, his hand tightening its grip on his shoulder as his mood darkened. It was difficult to keep his fingers from digging deep enough to give his brother a small taste of pain. Simon wondered if Gideon's sole purpose in life was to torment him.

"The point is," Simon said, "last night I was cursing the storm and all the problems and accidents it was causing, and this morning I look out the window and am blown away by the beauty it created. You always see the dark side of things. You always see manure as crap, and never as fertilizer."

Gideon squirmed under the pressure of Simon's steely grip and pointed remarks. "How was your date last night?" he asked, changing the subject to avoid the same old lecture. He had heard it a hundred times before.

"It was fine, but why the interest in my love life all of a sudden?" Simon asked, his mood and grip lightening.

"Well..." Gideon stammered. "I'm not getting anywhere with Jenny Bloom, and I thought Maureen might have a friend."

"I thought you were making some progress with Jenny," Simon replied.

"Progress?" Gideon asked. "I can barely summon the courage to say hello to her. She's caught me looking at her several times, and I think she knows I like her, but let's face it. What would a girl like Jenny want with someone like me?"

A wave of empathy for his brother washed over Simon McGee and for a brief moment he saw himself four years earlier. "You're too hard on yourself, Gideon. You see yourself as worthless so you act the part. How can you expect Jenny to like you when you don't like yourself?"

Gideon turned from the window and walked across the small room to his bed and sat down, his eyes seeing nothing but his size seven feet. "That's easy for you to say, Simon. Have you looked in a mirror lately? When I look, I want to shut off the lights."

Bill Marshall

"There's nothing wrong with your body or your looks. You see what you want to see," Simon said. "What you need is an attitude adjustment. Change your attitude and the reflection in the mirror will change."

"That's your standard line. It's like saying, 'don't worry'." Gideon looked away and scratched his name onto the flannel of his pajama leg. "Are you going to ask Maureen or not?"

Gideon and Simon turned as their ten-year-old sister entered their room.

"Good morning Simon. Good morning Gideon," Prudence said, standing in their doorway in her flannel nightgown. Prudence was the youngest McGee, a pretty girl whose sandy-blonde hair was worn in a pony tail tied with a yellow ribbon, just like her mother's. If Gideon held his arm out straight, she would just clear it without ducking. Her almond-brown eyes sparkled whenever she saw Gideon, for despite his surly attitude she loved him dearly. "Can I come in?"

"No," Gideon said.

"Of course you can, Prudence," Simon said, overruling his younger brother. "Have you looked outside yet?"

"Yes, but it's much prettier on your side of the house."

Prudence's room was across the hall, and her window faced east so that her view was into the sun. From her brother's side the ice-covered trees reflected the sun much like the full moon. It was always easier looking at the sun's reflection than it was gazing directly into it.

"What were you guys talking about?" Prudence asked, noticing the frown on Gideon's face.

"Girls," Simon said, his eyes drawn to the light red fingernail polish that was beginning to chip from his sister's delicate fingers.

7

"I'm a girl. What do you want to know?"

"You're too young to be of any help, Prudence," Gideon said, delighting in the look his words created on his sister's face.

Prudence stomped her feet and placed her hands on her hips, which at her age were no wider than her waist. "I'm ten years old, Gideon McGee, and I probably know a lot more about girls than you do. You're such a pain."

Prudence turned and left the room in a huff, a move she learned from watching her mother. It often made her father repent for some unseen wrongdoing that neither she nor her father knew he had committed.

"Why don't you lighten up on Prudence?" Simon asked in a voice more controlled than he felt. "Whether you know it or not, she loves you very much, although I'll never understand why."

"I haven't been sleeping well. That's all. Leave me alone."

"My pleasure, little brother."

"Don't call me little brother."

Simon stalked out of the room. Gideon, still seated on the edge of his bed, cupped his oval face in his hands and wondered, as usual, why life always dealt him deuces.

Chapter Two

The ice storm served to mark the end of Christmas break and the beginning of the second semester. For some, who saw the beauty the storm left behind, it was a good omen. Others, focusing on its destruction, saw it as a bad sign. Some saw crap, others, fertilizer. A few, a very few, saw the storm as both good and bad, much like a forest fire that on the surface appears to ravage nature, but upon deeper reflection merely prunes it, making way for new growth.

"I don't think there's anything more boring than washing dishes," Gideon said to his mother who was clearing the table of the dinner dishes. "Why can't we have a dish washer like normal people?"

Clara McGee had heard this complaint many times before. "I swear, Gideon McGee," she huffed. "If you had a dollar for every time you complained you'd be a rich boy. You could buy yourself a dishwasher for each day of the week."

Clara McGee was an attractive woman who had fully lived her thirty-six years and could still fit into her high school prom gown if an occasion ever arose for her to do so. Her straight blonde hair was cut just short enough to be worn in the pony tail that her daughter so loved. It required half the upkeep of the longer hair she preferred, and seemed a good compromise to getting a Bob cut. At thirty-six, Clara McGee was more concerned with the practical aspects of life than in pleasing herself before a mirror. She wouldn't admit it, but she was beautiful and very comfortable with her reflection in the mirror.

She placed her collection of dishes and utensils on the counter next to the sink and gave Gideon a quick kiss on the cheek.

"Mom!" Gideon complained, wiping the kiss with a dish rag. "I'm not five-years-old anymore." He loved her kisses, and would have been saddened had she not stuck to her usual routine of stealing one. It was a game they played. Each knew the rules, but never admitted to them. It was permissible for Clara to steal a kiss from her fourteen-year-old son, but open displays of affection were not allowed. Gideon learned early the cultural gender tabus.

"Mom?" Gideon asked, his voice hesitant and unsure, like a sky diver the moment before his first jump.

"Yes, Gideon," she replied, recognizing his change in tone.

"Do you ever think the world is out to get you? You know . . . like nothing goes your way. Even my birthday sucks."

"Gideon!" Clara McGee grabbed the dishrag from her son and swatted him with it. "December 26th is a perfect day for a birthday."

"Yeah, if you're born in some third world country where the average yearly income is two hundred dollars."

"What are you talking about?"

"It seems my whole life has been like having a birthday the day after Christmas. Shortchanged, you know."

"No!" his mother exclaimed. "I don't know, and I think you're dead wrong. There are four billion worlds out there, one for each of us and no two people see it the same way. If you're not happy with the world you have, how about seeing it in a different way?"

Gideon noticed the edge to his mother's voice and decided to tone down his own. "Well . . . maybe my life isn't that bad, but

10

sometimes it sure seems so. So how do I go about seeing the world differently?"

"The world I see is quite different from the world you see," his mother answered. "Take Elvis Presley for example."

"You take him," Gideon said, his face a scowl. "I can't stand him."

"That's my point exactly, Gideon. You and I look at the same man and we see two completely different people. I see the king of rock and roll, who might show up some day at a gas station or a Walmart, and you see some dead guy who used to sing a bunch of corny hick-songs.

"Or take football," his mother continued. "Norwich High played New London High for the championship last year, and New London won. For the New London fans it was a great day. They were happy, exuberant, and did a lot of celebrating that night. For the Norwich fans the day was a bust. You have your brother to attest to that. Same day, but seen differently by two groups of people."

"Yeah," Gideon said, refusing to understand and forgetting Simon's comments about manure. "But it was still the same day. I'm going to take a walk down by the pond. Where's the flash-light?"

"It's on the shelf over the washing machine, but be careful. I don't know how thick the ice is, so keep off the pond. Be back in an hour."

Gideon often took walks to the pond whenever there was something troubling him. He had named the small body of water Round Pond after its perfectly circular shape. The pond was a quarter mile from his home and sat like a teardrop on five acres of city property that abutted his land. From its grassy banks he could see the volunteer fire station only a hundred yards away. His parents played Bingo there every Tuesday night. Gideon thought taking a nap would be more exciting than Bingo, but kept his opinion to himself.

Gideon had been feeling unsettled since the ice storm three days earlier. He couldn't describe the feeling exactly, but sensed something was going to happen. His stomach felt as though he were dropping in an elevator, and the narrow path that he could usually walk blindfolded, now required his attention and the beam of his flashlight. His mother's explanation only served to heighten that feeling of being disconnected. If there were four billion worlds for four billion people, why was his so pitiful?

As he stood on the frozen banks of Round Pond his mind was assaulted with questions that seemed to come from somewhere other than from his own brain.

Why isn't life fair? Why did Simon get mom's looks and I got dad's? What did mom mean when she said we all see the world differently? Why can't we all be the same? These questions darted in and out of his mind like mice scurrying for cover at the flick of a light switch. These thoughts and his dreams were foreign to him and seemed as though they were injected into his mind by an invisible hypodermic needle. He wondered whose hand was on the syringe.

The siren at the fire station sounded, calling the volunteers to action, and jerking Gideon out of his thoughts. He looked at his Timex Ironman watch he just received for his birthday and pressed the indiglo button to illuminate the time. 9:03 p.m. appeared through the green indiglo haze. He had been gone for an hour and fifteen minutes, and yet it seemed like only a moment. Time, Gideon thought, what a chameleon.

Gideon was home by 9:30 p.m. and asleep by ten. He

wondered what dream would assail him tonight as he drifted further and further from consciousness. Recently he had become aware while dreaming that he was dreaming. It was like watching himself in a feature length movie. He knew he was in the audience, and what was happening on screen, although looking real, was merely a simulation.

The images began to come into focus. It was long ago in a far off land, an exotic land of wide plains and shallow seasonal lakes where the balance of nature remained undisturbed. A tiger came into view, long and lean, looking hungry and exhausted. It had been a harsh summer with little rain and even less food, and the female tiger hadn't eaten in weeks. She had little strength left and her unborn cub was about to arrive.

In the distance she spied a small band of goats nibbling on the roots of some long-gone prairie grass. She summoned the last of her ebbing strength and made a wild charge at the herd. A small kid standing near its mother seemed the most likely target and the tiger focused her energy in a last ditch effort to save herself and her unborn cub. She leaped at the kid, but the effort was too much and her heart gave out in mid-flight.

The force of her body hitting the ground was enough to send the cub within her into the light of day. It was born as though shot from a canon and landed in the midst of the band of goats. Surprised at first, they were timid in approaching the startled cub, but soon overcame their fear and eventually welcomed the cub into their band as one of their own.

As time marched inexorably along its path, the tiger grew to think of itself as a goat. It grazed on grass like a goat. It ran from predators like a goat. It even bleated like a goat. The goats, for their part, forgot the tiger was a tiger, although they often wondered why he looked so different from the rest of them. Gideon knew that in this dream he was the tiger-goat, but as yet was unable to make the connection between the metaphors of his dream and the reality of his life.

One day, while the herd of goats was grazing lazily near a small pond, they were surprised by a full-grown male tiger. Just as his long sabered teeth were about to break the neck of an old crippled goat he saw, and then heard, the bleating of the tiger-goat. He dropped his prey as if it were a hot ember, and looked in amazement at the freak of nature.

What he saw was a distorted reflection of himself. The tiger-goat looked like a tiger, although a little smaller and not as well muscled, but didn't act like a tiger. The old male, a veteran of many hunts and fights for dominance, let loose a kingly roar. The tiger-goat bleated his reply. "Ba-a-a-a."

"What are you?" the old tiger asked in a fury.

"Ba-a-a-a," the tiger-goat replied. "I am a goat."

"You are not a goat!" roared the tiger. "You are a tiger like me. Well, maybe not just like me, but you are a tiger."

"Ba-a-a-a."

The tiger was so infuriated by this reply he grabbed the tiger-goat by the scruff of the neck with his mouth and dragged him to the nearby pond. "Look," he ordered. "Look at your reflection. Is that the face of a goat?" He forced the tiger-goat's face toward the water.

"Ba-a-a-a," the tiger-goat said. "I look like you."

"You not only look like me, but the same blood that courses through my veins, also runs through yours." The kingly tiger dropped the tiger-goat into the pond, then went to finish-off the wounded goat he had dropped from his mouth only a few moments ago. As easily as a man carries a briefcase, he carried the carcass over to the stunned tiger-goat.

"Have you ever eaten meat?" the tiger asked in disdain. Blood dripped from his jowls as he dropped the dead goat and tore at its flesh with his massive teeth.

"Why would I eat meat," the tiger-goat replied, "when there's plenty of grass?"

A roar went out over the plains the likes of which the animals never heard before. An eerie silence fell over the land. The tiger grabbed the tiger-goat on the back of its neck and forced his face into the fresh kill.

"Eat! Taste!" the tiger roared. "This is what you are meant to eat. A tiger is what you are meant to be."

As the blood of the goat entered the tiger-goat's mouth he felt a surge of power that began at the tip of its tail and moved with ever-increasing speed through his body. He felt it enter his mouth and with a joy he had not known before, he proclaimed with a roar to all who would hear. "I am a tiger, hear me roar."

Chapter Three

H ello," said Mrs. McGee, mildly annoyed that the phone tore her away from Peter Jennings and the evening News. She reluctantly swung her feet to the floor and lifted herself from the green plaid Herculon couch that was six steps from the kitchen and the only phone in the house.

"Hello. This is Jenny Bloom. May I speak to Gideon, please?"

"Oh, hello Jenny. This is Gideon's mother. We haven't met, but I know your mother. I understand she was in an accident a couple of weeks ago. I hope she's feeling better."

"She's much better. Thank you, Mrs. McGee," Jenny said. "Her arm was broken, but it could have been much worse. The man who hit her was drunk and it was only luck that saved her. The car was totaled. He hit mom's car at the rear passengers' door on the driver's side. Two feet to the left and . . . well, mom was lucky."

"Well, I'm glad to hear it wasn't more serious," Gladys McGee said. She felt uncomfortable and at a loss for words to describe adequately how she felt, for her mother had been killed by a drunk driver ten years earlier. "Hold on a minute, and I'll get Gideon."

Mrs. McGee put the phone down slowly as she remembered the pain of ten years ago. She walked to Gideon's room, for she hated yelling and refused to do so even though the walk down the hall was inconvenient.

"Gideon," she said, knocking on his door. "Telephone. It's Jenny Bloom."

He had expected Jenny to call since being teamed with her for a science project that afternoon by Mrs. Gibson. Gideon practiced all afternoon what he would say to Jenny, and found she made him more nervous than blocking a two-hundred-pound defensive tackle. He threw open the door to his bedroom and nearly knocked his mother over as he raced for the phone.

"Hello," he said before the phone was halfway to his mouth.

"Hello? Gideon? I can hardly hear you," Jenny said. The sound of her voice made him dizzy.

"This is Gideon. We have a problem with the cord sometimes. It's one of those old dial phones." He lied about the cord, but not about the style of phone. Mr. McGee couldn't see spending good money on a new phone just so he could push buttons and save three seconds in dialing up a number. "I guess you're calling about Mrs. Gibson's science project." Gideon couldn't imagine her calling him for any other reason.

"Yes. I tried to talk to you after class, but you rushed off so fast I didn't get a chance."

Gideon bolted out of the class at the sound of the bell. He couldn't speak to Jenny Bloom without first rehearsing what he would say. He had to avoid her, for something as difficult as talking to the girl he liked required preparation, and as with most things in his life he was not prepared.

"I had a meeting with my guidance counselor and I didn't want to be late," Gideon lied.

"You know, Gideon, I never thanked you for the Coke you got me at lunch just before Christmas break. I was so shocked. I was dying of thirst and didn't have a cent on me, and then you show up with a Coke. I was speechless."

Gideon overheard Jenny complain to Barbara Howser how she'd kill for a Coke, that she just finished gym and her mouth was as dry as straw. He rushed to the soda machine, deposited three quarters, then rushed back with the Coke.

"You looked thirsty," Gideon said, fumbling for words.

"Whatever," Jenny said. "Have you given any thought to our science project? It can also be a paper, you know? I've been thinking we could do something about the environment."

"That's a good idea," Gideon said, not wanting to offend Jenny. "But don't you think a lot of the other teams will be doing something on the environment too?"

"Yeah, you're probably right, but what else is there?"

"This will probably sound stupid to you, but how about doing a paper on dreams?"

"That doesn't sound stupid at all," Jenny said excitedly. "How did you ever come up with that idea? It's great!"

"I don't know," he said, shrugging his shoulders as though Jenny was there to see. "It just popped into my mind. But I've been having a lot of strange dreams lately, and I thought it might be fun to find out about them."

"This is such a coincidence," Jenny said. "Just the other day Barbara Howser told me about a strange dream she had."

"Oh? What was it about?" Gideon asked, not really caring about Barbara Howser's dream, but wanting to drag out the conversation.

"I promised her I wouldn't tell, but it had to do with a tug of war."

Gideon's heart raced, much like it did just before the snap of the football in a game. A sense of urgency came over him that

18

he neither understood nor cared to understand. "When did she have the dream?" he asked, his voice harsh and insistent.

"Why do you want to know?"

"Just tell me . . . please!"

"Well, she told me about it on Monday, so she must have had the dream on Sunday, the night of the ice storm."

Gideon stopped breathing and his heart seemed to move from his chest to his ears.

"Gideon? Are you there?" Jenny asked.

"Yes . . . yes, I'm here. It must be the phone line again."

"What is it?" Jenny asked, not believing him this time. "What's the matter?"

"I had a tug-of-war dream the next day. You've got to tell me about Barbara's dream," Gideon demanded, forgetting his shyness and whom he was talking to.

"I'll tell you, but if you ever tell Barbara I'll never speak to you again."

"Promise. My lips are sealed," Gideon said. He made a mental note never to tell Jenny a secret.

Jenny launched into the telling of Barbara Howser's dream, while Gideon sat transfixed to the receiver of the beige phone. "The dream was very strange. You were triplets."

"What do you mean, 'I was triplets,'? Are you saying her dream was about me?"

"That's what I said, and I didn't say twins. Did I? I said triplets, and each one was different. One was dressed completely in black and wore a scowl on his face. He was a shadowy creature and gave Barbara the creeps. The second Gideon was in white, and his face was an ear-to-ear grin, like the Cheshire Cat in Alice in Wonderland. He gave Barbara the creeps as much as the shadow-Gideon did. The third Gideon glowed a sort of golden color, and

19

Barbara said she was drawn to him in the most pleasant sort of way."

"What were they doing?" Gideon asked, barely able to contain his curiosity.

"They were having a tug of war with a golden rope. Actually, the black Gideon and the white Gideon were having the tug of war. The golden Gideon was in the center and with each hand held a luminous knotted rope that the other two Gideons were tugging on."

"Were they saying anything?" Gideon asked.

"The angry, scowling Gideon kept shouting, 'I hate you', while the mindlessly smiling Gideon answered, 'I love you.' The golden Gideon seemed perfectly at peace and said nothing."

"Who won the tug of war?" Gideon asked, impatient to hear the conclusion.

"That was the odd part," Jenny said, closing her eyes for a moment and reflecting on the dream. "The golden Gideon, with ever-so-subtle finger movements, drew the other two Gideons toward him. The rope seemed to disappear into the golden Gideon's hand as he drew the other two closer and closer to him. And as the smiling and the scowling Gideons came closer to the peaceful Gideon their shouting grew softer."

Gideon waited for Jenny to continue, but all he heard was silence. It hung in the phone's receiver like an angry wasp, stinging his ear. "So?" he yelled. "Don't you dare leave me hanging like this. What happened next?"

"Barbara woke up. And that's it," Jenny said. "The dream ended there, with no winner of the tug of war." Jenny couldn't understand Gideon's agitation. After all, she thought, it was only a dream. "What's the big deal about Barbara's dream?" she asked.

"I had a dream just like it," he said, and began his story, amazed that two people could have such similar dreams. "In my dream the tug of war wasn't between people, it was between circles, one a half circle and the other a full circle.

"The dream started as an image of one circle, half black and half white. Gradually the circle began to split and separate down the middle where the black and white meet.

"As they separated, the space between them filled with gold until it became a complete circle with the black and white halves some distance to the right and left of the middle circle that was now completely gold."

"That doesn't sound like a tug of war to me," Jenny said. "The two half circles and the gold circle aren't connected from what you've said so far."

"That's right," Gideon said. "The black and white halves kept moving farther and farther away from the gold center until finally the gold circle shot out two golden threads that attached to the black and white halves.

"The two halves began to vibrate as though they were trying to continue their separation from the gold center, but the thread stopped their progress.

"Gradually the gold circle began to reel in the black and white halves, and, as they approached, the gold circle grew larger.

"With what seemed to be one great final effort the gold circle drew the two halves into itself. As the last of the black and white halves disappeared into the gold, the gold exploded. The circle grew in all directions and seemed to expand into the size of a Galaxy. It continued to grow, gobbling up galaxy after galaxy when I finally woke up."

Jenny had the ending of Barbara Howser's dream. She knew from Gideon's dream that the golden Gideon would have won the tug of war, and that he would have grown by absorbing the black and white Gideons. Jenny didn't understand the meaning of it all, but was determined to find out.

"What do you think it all means, Gideon?" Jenny asked.

"How should I know?" Gideon scoffed, thinking her question ridiculous. "Until you mentioned Barbara's dream, I had forgotten about mine. I've never paid much attention to dreams, and except for an occasional nightmare I didn't think I dreamed at all. That is, until two weeks ago."

Jenny sat thinking for a moment and then asked, "Do you know Susan Spiro?"

"Not very well. She's in our Algebra I class, isn't she? What about her?"

"Well . . . I've known her for years, and we're quite good friends. Her father's a shrink, and I remember Sue telling me once that he works with people's dreams."

"Yeah, so?" Gideon asked, not yet catching where Jenny was going with this train of thought.

"So maybe we could kill two birds with one stone," Jenny answered. "We could find out some things about dreams for our paper, and maybe discover what your dream means at the same time."

"I don't know if I want to find out what my dream means. What if it's something bad?"

"What if it is?" Jenny shot back. "You can't go through life without some bad happening."

"Yeah, but I've had more than my fair share."

"Are you blind?" Jenny asked.

"What do you mean?"

"I mean just what I said. Are you blind?"

"No," Gideon answered.

"Tim Chimera is blind. Are you deaf?"

"No."

"Laura Harken is deaf. Are you mentally handicapped?"

"Sometimes I wonder," Gideon said, laughing. "Enough already. I get your point."

"If I can arrange a meeting with Dr. Spiro this Saturday can you make it?"

"I think so," Gideon said, knowing he rarely had plans for the weekend. "I don't have anything planned, yet."

"Good. I'll call Sue now and let you know tomorrow in Mr. Numer's class. Is that okay?"

"Sure. That would be fine."

"Great. Then I'll talk to you tomorrow. Goodbye Gideon."

"Goodbye Jenny. See you tomorrow."

Gideon's loud yelp as he hung up the phone startled his mother in the next room. The dizziness he felt when he first picked up the phone returned, and he had to steady himself on the kitchen table. He wondered if this happened to every boy.

"Gideon," she said. "You sound like you just won the lottery. Did Jenny promise you a dishwasher?"

"Really funny, mom," Gideon replied, embarrassed he was so careless with his emotions. "But maybe my luck's about to change." He walked back to his room and fell asleep that night hoping Jenny would appear in his dreams.

Chapter Four

S aturday morning Gideon awoke as the sun peeked above the horizon and shot its fingers into his room. Normally he could be found with the shades drawn and the covers pulled over his head until ten or eleven A.M., but this day was special. He was to meet Jenny Bloom at Dr. Spiro's home at eleven o'clock. The day held the promise that the night kept from him. The dawn sky was clear and the full moon was still visible in the west as the sun exploded in the east.

Simon agreed to drive his increasingly hyper brother to Goldman Avenue for the interview with Dr. Spiro. By the time they left their house, the rest of the family was glad to be rid of the youngest male McGee.

"Calm down, Gideon," Simon said, as he maneuvered the family Ford around the numerous potholes in the dirt road. "You're so nervous your face is starting to break out."

"No way," Gideon said in alarm. He jerked the rear-view mirror in his direction and checked his reflection. "Where?" he asked, turning his face from side to side. "I don't see any zits."

"Right there," Simon said, pointing in the general direction of his brother's face. A large smile spread across his own at the thought of his brother's unease.

"Where? I can't see it." Gideon frantically moved his head from side to side in a futile attempt to discover the imaginary irruption.

"Relax, Gideon," Simon laughed. "I'm just jerking your chain. What's the street number on Goldman? I forgot."

"Forty-four Goldman Avenue. Jenny said it's halfway down the street on the right, an old red colonial. You're such a jerk, Simon." Gideon turned the rear-view mirror back in his brother's direction.

"Sorry, little brother," Simon said. "I couldn't help myself. You've been driving everyone crazy all morning."

"Yeah? And I suppose you were Joe Cool on your first date, Mr. know-it-all."

"This isn't exactly a date, Gideon," Simon said. The ease with which Simon sailed through life made it nearly impossible for him to understand Gideon's plight.

"It's the closest thing to one I've ever had, so be quiet. You're making me nervous." Gideon's foot tapped out Morse code on the Taurus floorboard.

"You're making yourself nervous. Forget about Jenny for a minute and think about what you're going to ask Dr. Spiro."

Gideon and Simon rode in silence for the next few minutes. Simon listened to Boyz II Men on WRX radio, and Gideon listened to his thoughts. He knew nothing about dreams and believed the sitcoms on T.V. that they were the result of one too many bean burritos. He'd just have to depend on Jenny to ask the right questions while he worked the tape recorder. Life was just too stressful to cope with sometimes, he thought.

"There it is," Simon said as he applied the brakes on the aging blue Taurus. "Big house. There must be a lot of psychos around Norwich."

"Yeah, and you're one of them. I think I'll ask Dr. Spiro if he takes any charity cases." Gideon dashed from the car, barely dodging Simon's fist that crashed into his recently vacated seat.

"You're the one that needs a shrink, you twerp," Simon yelled after his brother whose smile was his victory sign. Gideon relished these small victories as a poor child savors a square of chocolate.

"Pick me up at twelve o'clock," Gideon shouted back. "Don't forget."

The walk up the brick walkway to the Spiro's front door seemed a mile long, and with each step, Gideon's heart picked up its pace. He noticed the large horseshoe door-knocker on the front door just as Sue Spiro swung it open.

"Hi Gideon," she said. "Jenny's already here. Come on in." Sue was a tall girl and her brown eyes were level with Gideon's. Her smile was quick and broad and came from her heart. If Gideon allowed the thought, he could almost imagine she was happy to see him.

As he followed her through the long hallway to the study where he was to meet with Dr. Spiro his eyes were caught by a large painting on the wall. It was a circle filled with what looked like two curved teardrops, one black and one white. At the center of the white teardrop was a black eye, and at the center of the black teardrop was a white eye.

"That's the symbol of the Tao," Sue said, happy that Gideon noticed her favorite wall-hanging. "Tao means the 'Way' in Chinese." Her long slender finger traced the symbol in the painting.

"The way of what?" Gideon asked, absently fingering his face for the imaginary zit.

"The 'Way' of life," Sue said as though it was as plain as the small nose on her face.

"They look like two fish kissing each other's tail," Gideon replied.

"You're right, Gideon, they do. They're supposed to

represent a world of opposites. We think black is the opposite of white, but the believer's in the Tao say that it's all mixed together. That's why each fish has its opposite's color at its very center."

Gideon thought of his dream and the black and white circles, and it occurred to him that there might be a connection between this symbol of the 'Tao' and the symbols of his dream. His finger drifted to his ear in search of a fingernail's worth of wax, and the thought left his head.

"Come along, Gideon," Sue said, not noticing his catch. "Jenny and my father are waiting for you."

The door to Dr. Spiro's study was open, and, as he crossed the threshold, Gideon's long straight nose sniffed a cloud of pipe smoke. The walls were lined with books, more books than Gideon had ever seen outside a library. He couldn't imagine anyone ever wanting to read so many books. Dr. Spiro was seated in a dark black leather recliner, and as he stood to greet Gideon it became obvious from whom Sue inherited her height.

Gideon's eyes, directed straight ahead, gazed directly at Dr. Spiro's protruding Adam's Apple. The psychiatrist stood at least six feet four inches tall in a body that seemed more suited to a weight lifter than a man of the mind.

"Hello, Gideon," he said, extending his spade-sized hand. "I'm Ben Spiro. Jenny's been bringing me up to speed on your dream project and more interestingly to me, the dream you and Barbara Howser had a week ago. Please, have a seat."

Gideon took the only other seat available, which was next to Jenny on an overstuffed couch. He was grateful for the lack of additional seating as he slowly sank into place.

"Hi, Gideon," Jenny said, shooting a broad smile in his direction. "I'm glad you remembered the tape recorder."

Dr. Spiro sat down again in his recliner, and reached for

his pipe on the desk. The room smelled like a tobacco barn.

"Do you mind if I smoke?" he asked. "I tend to think better with this pipe in my mouth."

"No, go ahead," Gideon said, thinking that Dr. Spiro must do a lot of thinking. "That is if it's all right with you, Jenny."

Ignoring Jenny, Dr. Spiro lit his pipe.

"Dreams are my favorite subject," he said, in-between puffs. "They can tell us a great deal about ourselves."

"I always thought dreams were nonsense," Gideon responded. "Caused by one too many bean burritos."

"To most people today, they are nonsense. But it hasn't always been that way. Before the modern age people placed a great deal of importance on dreams."

"But isn't that old fashioned?" Jenny asked, looking to Gideon for support.

"Old," Dr. Spiro answered, "but not old fashioned. It's only been about three hundred years that we've stopped listening to our dreams, ever since Isaac Newton, the great mathematician and philosopher."

"What did he have to do with it?" Gideon asked, being drawn into the conversation by Dr. Spiro's easy way, but slightly distracted by Jenny's nearness to him on the couch, and the cloud of smoke that was quickly filling the room.

"Newton started us on the path of measuring and quantifying nature. You know. Every effect has a cause. We stopped believing in dreams, because we stopped believing that there might be a reality beyond what our five senses told us. What we couldn't see or measure gradually faded from our experience."

"Before two weeks ago I hardly ever dreamed," Gideon said. "If dreams are so important why don't I dream every night?"

"You do," Dr. Spiro answered. "You just don't remember them. There's all kind of research available now that tells us all human beings dream every night. In fact, if your dreaming is interrupted night after night, you will become psychotic or, as you call it, crazy."

"How can dreams be important of we can't even remember them?" Jenny asked. Gideon nodded his head.

"Do you have to know how an engine works in order to drive a car? Do you have to know how an energy plant converts oil to electricity to enjoy its benefits? Dreams work in the unconscious, Jenny, that part of your Being you're unaware of.

"Your mind is much like an iceberg," Dr. Spiro continued. "The part you see above the water line is like your conscious mind, the part of your mind that is aware. The greater part of the iceberg, however, lies beneath the water line and is invisible."

"What does the ocean that the iceberg floats in stand for?" Gideon asked, surprised that he should even think of such a question. It wasn't like him, and he wondered where it came from. Maybe it came from the same place his dreams came from, he thought.

"Some might say the ocean stands for God," Dr. Spiro said.

"When we remember our dreams," Jenny said, "why are they so strange? Why are they hard to understand?"

"Because they speak to us in symbols. The images you see in the dreams stand for something else."

"But if they're important to us why don't they just come out and say what they mean instead of making us guess?" Gideon asked.

Jenny looked at Gideon, impressed by his question. Without knowing she slid her body a fraction of an inch closer to him.

29

"Great question, Gideon," Dr. Spiro said. "But to answer it you need to understand a little about how I see the world and the part we play in it." He placed his pipe, a white meerschaum, in the ashtray. "I believe we are much, much more than what our five senses perceive.

"For instance, in my practice I'm seeing a young man with multiple personality disorder. Do you know what that is?"

"No," Jenny said. Gideon shook his head.

"It's when several distinct personalities exist in the same person. That is to say, what appears physically to be one person is actually several different people in one body. In this particular case, the individual I'm speaking of has sugar diabetes in his primary personality for which he must take regular insulin injections to control. His secondary personality is completely free of the disease. One of his minor personalities is a juvenile delinquent, and I've actually seen his face break out in pimples as he assumes this identity."

"How can that happen?" Jenny asked, her eyebrows arched in disbelief.

"What we know of nature says that it can't happen, just as what we know of nature says miracles can't happen. But they do, and they happen all the time. A miracle doesn't break the laws of nature, but it does go against what we know of nature.

"Have you ever seen the National Geographic T.V. show where people walk barefoot through red-hot coals without even blistering their feet?" Dr. Spiro asked.

"Yeah," Gideon said. "No way. It had to be a trick, like something a magician would do."

"It's real," Dr. Spiro assured him. "I've been present during a fire walk, and I can promise you, it is very real. You can't

30

believe it, because you have a particular view of reality that this event doesn't fit into. You must remember that your beliefs about reality are not necessarily attributes of reality.

"What I'm getting at is that who we really are, our real self, or soul, if you will, is much larger than we suspect, and we exist in some way in other forms outside of our bodies. Some call it Heaven, some Nirvana, but it's another form of existence.

"Our dreams speak to us in symbols and images, to answer your question, Gideon, because it's a common universal language."

"Let me see if I have this straight," Jenny said. "It's like me trying to communicate with someone who speaks only Swahili. Words won't work, but I might be able to get my point across by drawing pictures. Is that right?"

"That's close enough," Dr. Spiro said. "And the images the dreams use invariably relate to energies within ourselves that we've repressed. Dreams are often compensations for those parts of ourselves that we refuse to live out in our daily lives."

Gideon couldn't contain his curiosity any longer. The information Dr. Spiro presented did nothing but heighten his interest in his own dream.

"What about my dream?" Gideon asked. "You know. The one Jenny told you about. What does it mean?"

"I can't tell you what it means, Gideon. Only you can determine that. But I can guide you toward finding your own meaning. It seems to me that yours was an important dream, what we head shrinkers call a big dream."

"What do you mean, a big dream?" Gideon asked.

"It deals with more than just your day-to-day living. The symbols it uses, especially the gold circle, are universal and generally refer to... "

With Gideon on the edge of his seat, the phone rang,

interrupting Dr. Spiro in mid-sentence. Gideon could tell from Dr. Spiro's set jaw and tightened lips that there was some sort of an emergency. He reinserted his pipe and bit down hard.

"Okay, officer," Dr. Spiro said into the phone, his pipe bobbing from the corner of his mouth like a feather on a turbulent sea. "Don't approach him. Keep him talking, and I'll be there in ten minutes."

Dr. Spiro hung up the phone. "Sorry, guys," he said. "We'll have to finish this some other time. I've got an emergency."

Dr. Spiro was out the door and out of the house before either Gideon or Jenny could say a word. Gideon's dream would have to wait for another time.

Chapter Five

S imon felt the thrashing before he heard the screams. It was a gurgling sound he heard first, as though someone was drowning. Then came a howl of terror. Simon threw off his covers and jumped the six feet to the floor, landing hard on his heels.

"Gideon!" Simon said, shaking his shivering brother. "Wake up. You're having a bad dream."

"What?" Gideon asked, gradually awakening from a deep sleep and realizing he had been in the middle of a nightmare.

"Come on..." Simon shook his brother again. "Wake up. You've had a nightmare." He wondered what junk food his brother had eaten to cause such a reaction.

It was two A.M. Sunday morning. The room was as black as a Kentucky cave at midnight. Gideon could hear and feel his brother, but his body was formless, blending with the color of night.

"Man! I'm freezing," Gideon said, his body shaking as though he had gone for a swim in a glacier field lake. "Why is it so cold in here?"

Simon felt the goose bumps on Gideon's arms, and had he not been in the same room with his shivering brother he would have sworn Gideon just left a meat freezer. "That must have been some dream," he said. "I've never seen you like this before. What happened?"

Gideon stopped shaking for a moment as he tried to remember. "I was falling through a funnel that looked like a tornado. It was blacker than the pupil of my eye, and cold, so cold." His shivering increased.

"It was just a dream," Simon said, trying to soothe his brother. "Go back to sleep now. It's over."

Simon tucked-in Gideon then felt his way to the linen closet in the hall for an extra blanket for his still-shivering brother. By the time he returned Gideon was asleep. Simon covered his brother and went back to bed.

*   *   *

By the time Gideon woke up five hours later he had largely forgotten his dream, but an unsettled feeling lingered, a sense of foreboding. The January warm-snap continued, but did little to diminish the chill that remained in Gideon McGee's bones. It was like a cold virus that nothing could touch but time. He needed to get out of the house, and when Prudence asked to join him for a walk in the woods, he accepted.

"You're being really quiet this morning," Prudence said as they entered the path through the woods to Round Pond. "You haven't said a single mean thing to me and it's almost noon."

"You talk too much," Gideon said, wanting more to listen to the crunch of the dead leaves under his feet than to his sister's voice. He was glad she was with him, but needed the silence.

"There's the Gideon I know," Prudence said, scrunching up her face at his response, but out of his line of sight.

Gideon was tired. Prudence could see it in the slump of his shoulders and the downward cast of his eyes. His inner world reflected itself in the way he carried himself in the outer world. Gideon McGee was tired of complaining. He was tired of feeling

34

that life was nothing more than good luck or bad luck, and that his was usually bad. He was tired of seeing his life governed by the whims of others. He was tired of all these things, but didn't know it. What Gideon knew was that something strange was happening to him, something beyond his comprehension. As he walked with his sister to Round Pond he felt like a marionette, and wondered who the puppeteer was.

The ice from the storm of a week ago had long since melted, and the woods were dry and brown, deep in their winter hibernation. Round Pond, looking like a perfect circular diamond, loomed before them. Prudence broke into a run.

"It's so beautiful, Gideon. Come on," Prudence yelled in a voice filled with the wonder and excitement of a ten year old, a voice that indicated no awareness of the critically thinned ice.

By the time Gideon snapped out of his dark brooding Prudence was at the edge of the ice-covered pond, and fear grabbed her brother by the throat.

"Get off the ice Pru! Get off! It's too thin!" Gideon screamed. He broke into a run, his legs turning faster than he thought possible, while his sister glided to the center of the pond.

"Don't be silly," she yelled. "Look! It's holding me just fine." To prove her point Prudence McGee began jumping as if on an invisible pogo stick . On the fourth jump she disappeared.

Gideon dove belly first onto the ice as though thrown by an invisible hand. He slid twenty feet before coming to a stop, still thirty feet from the black hole through which Prudence disappeared. He snaked forward on his belly, spreading his weight over a larger area and reducing his risk of falling through. Prudence's head popped above the surface of the ice like a fishing bob, a look of terror frozen on her face.

"Gideon!" she screamed between coughs that sprayed the

air with forty-degree pond water. Prudence managed to get her arms onto the ice, but the cold water brought on a sleep-like state that turned her spindly muscles into oatmeal. She was too weak save herself. Only her eyes reached out to her brother.

"Grab my hand, Pru," Gideon said, extending his straining arm toward her. He was plastered to the ice like paint on a wall, flat on his belly, and uncaring of the danger he was in. Prudence was too weak to speak, but her eyes spoke for her. Gideon knew the look, for he had it in his own eyes only a few short hours ago as he spiraled down a dark tunnel in his nightmare. The memory flooded him with a will to succeed.

With an effort he thought only his older brother could muster, Gideon grabbed hold of Prudence's small cold hand. From his position he didn't have the leverage or the angle that would allow him to pull her out. He had to stand up.

Gideon heard the low-pitched growl of cracking ice and time stood still as he saw himself plunge into the black water of Round Pond. With a presence of mind that seemed not his own, he realized that time was short and that his sister's life depended upon his quick and decisive action. As his head resurfaced Gideon McGee grabbed his sister by the waist. He gasped for air and with a prayer on his lips threw Prudence out of her watery grave and onto the ice.

"Stay on your stomach, Pru!" Gideon screamed. "Crawl to the near-bank and get help at the fire station. Hurry!"

Gideon attempted to pull himself out of the water, but his weight was too much for the thin ice to support. His body grew numb, and his mind weary. Thick winter clothing, soaked with ice-water, sealed his fate. Gideon's mind drifted between reality and dream. The world slowed down, as though he and all that he surveyed were part of a slow-motion movie. His voice dragged like a tape on a Walkman whose batteries could no longer hold a charge.

"Hurry...Pru..." The words oozed out like cold molasses, his mouth numbed like the rest of his body. Novocaine could not have done a better job.

The sun's light began to dim as though a full eclipse was in progress. As the last of the sun's light faded from Gideon's mind, he saw his sister reach the bank and race toward the fire house a hundred yards away.

Gideon felt nothing. A peace came over him as he slowly sank to the bottom of the shallow pond. Ten feet above, like a halo, stood the hole through which he fell. Suddenly a light appeared. Could it be that his rescuers had arrived so soon, he thought. Then, through the opening in the ice there appeared a Being-of-light, that floated down toward Gideon's still body.

"Do not be afraid, Gideon," the Being-of-light said. He was as bright as a thousand flood lights and difficult to look at.

"Who are you?" Gideon asked, surprised at his own calm until he noticed he was floating beside the Being-of-light, breathing easily, and looking down at his body.

"My name is Zacharaias, but you may call me Zack."

"I didn't ask what your name is. I asked who you are, what you are. What are you?"

"Your people call me a guardian angel, others call me a spirit guide. The name is not important. I have been with you since your birth. We're a team, so to speak."

"Am I... dead?" Gideon asked, with no more concern than he'd have when asking about the weather.

"The choice is yours," Zacharaias replied. "No one dies before their time, but before you make your decision you must accompany me on a journey. I will show you things that will make your passage through life less rocky, if you decide to live."

Gideon was at peace, maybe for the fist time in his conscious life. He trusted this Zacharaias, whose form was beginning to coalesce within the light. He was old, but not like the old people he knew. There was a youthfulness to him like that seen in a playful old dog. But it was Zack's eyes that won over Gideon McGee. They were the eyes of someone who no longer searches, the eyes of a man who has found what he was looking for, the eyes of peace and compassion, the eyes of knowing and love. Gideon fell under their spell.

"Where will you take me?" Gideon asked, staring down at his lifeless body, unconcerned.

"We shall visit several realities," Zack answered. "The first is the realm of the 'Gatekeeper.' From there we shall travel to the world of 'What is Good? What is Bad?' Our third sojourn will take us to the land of the 'Tree Clingers' and finally, our most important stop, 'The World of No Opposites.'"

Gideon was not completely ignorant of the effects of time on a body lying ten feet under water that was a heart-stopping 40 degrees.

" Uh...that sounds like it will take a long time," Gideon said nervously. "Won't my body die?"

Realizing that neither Gideon nor any human could understand that time existed only in their universe, Zacharaias extended his arm and pointed at Gideon's lifeless body. From the tip of his long bony finger shot a beam of golden light that surrounded the body that lay at the bottom of Round Pond like a sunken ship. From his physical body to his light body ran a silver thread.

38

"Have no fear, Gideon," Zack said. "Nothing shall happen to your body until you have decided to either complete your work here or move on."

Gideon felt as he did many years ago as his mother rocked him in her arms, and sang him a lullaby to soothe his raging fever. He felt safe and loved in the presence of Zacharaias and was tempted to have him cut the silver thread. But the vision of him in his mother's arms reminded him that he might be able to recapture that feeling on earth.

"When do we leave?" Gideon asked.

"Take hold of my hand," Zacharaias commanded, extending his glowing left hand to Gideon.

No sooner had Gideon taken hold of his guardian's hand than they began rising out of Round Pond, slowly at first, but then with ever-increasing speed. Gideon looked down and saw his body surrounded by the golden light and from it to his new light-body ran the silver thread, no thicker than the edge of a razor blade.

"Is there any part of your home that you would like to visit before we begin?" Zack asked. "Your home is very large, much larger than you imagine."

"Larger than you Imagine?" Gideon repeated. "What do you mean?"

Zacharaias was a master teacher, spending thousands of lifetimes traveling the universes, imparting his knowledge and wisdom. He began his first lesson. "In 1492 you thought the earth to be flat and the heavens to be filled with seven thousand stars that you could see with your naked eye. That flat plate was your home and the stars were out there." Zacharaias pointed to the heavens that both he and his traveling partner were fast approaching.

"In your time the earth has expanded to the dimensions of

a globe, and the heavens are populated by trillions upon trillions of stars, more than your computers could ever calculate. Your earth is larger now, but you are more crowded than ever. You refuse to see that your real home is eighteen trillion galaxies big. You are made of stardust yet you insist upon seeing yourself as puny, insignificant beings."

Zack held his thumb and forefinger together so that the slimmest filament of light passed through. "Come!" he commanded. "I am going to show you your home."

Gideon floated alongside his newly discovered friend and held tightly to his hand. Suddenly his concept of speed, travel and time were challenged to the limits of his imagination. The speed of light appeared as sluggish as a horse-drawn cart in comparison to the rate at which he and Zack were hurtling through the universe. Stars, even galaxies, streaked by in a kaleidoscope of blurred colors.

"How can we be going so fast?" Gideon asked, stunned by the ease with which all the physical laws he knew were broken.

"This is how the exploration of your home is to be done, Gideon," Zack replied. "We're actually traveling at a snail's pace due to your inexperience with thought-travel."

"Thought travel?" Gideon asked.

"Yes. In the future you need only think of where you wish to be, and you are there. You see, Gideon, you continue to see yourselves as a mere hodgepodge of cells and matter that through some cosmic coincidence learned how to think. The reality is that you are a consciousness, that is to say, a mind, that has learned to create a body. You are energy.

"You are much like the light bulb. What is important about the light bulb is not the glass or the filament that carries the light.

40

It is the light itself."

"This has got to be a dream," Gideon said, looking back to see if the silver thread was still attached. "As a matter of fact, this is more weird than any dream I've ever had. Where are you taking me?"

"We're going to the planet Moebius, in a galaxy its inhabitants have named Spiral. Next to your planet Earth, Moebius is the most beautiful planet in this universe." Zack turned his head slightly to the left and pointed. "There it is now."

Suspended in the black void of space, as though from an invisible thread, was Moebius, the second most beautiful planet in the Universe. It was a world much like Earth in size and color. The skin of Moebius was splashed with different shadings of blues, browns, greens and whites. As Zacharaias and Gideon slowed to a more reasonable space\time speed, Moebius came into sharp focus.

"This is great," Gideon said, feeling much as he does when around Jenny Bloom. "I feel like an eagle. How do I steer myself?"

"Just think of where you want to go," Zack replied. "It's a lot like flying a plane, but without the rudder and ailerons. Thought-travel is tricky at first, because you're so used to moving across distances. You see yourself moving from point A to point B by moving across space and by taking a certain amount of time. In advanced thought-travel no time lapses between the thought of where you want to be and being there."

Gideon looked down on Moebius and decided to visit a kidney-shaped continent colored in greens and browns and a few specks of white that looked like bird droppings. His attention was drawn to the white, and no sooner had he focused his attention on it than he appeared directly above the snow-capped peaks of a mountain range.

"Sh..." Gideon caught himself. "I mean Wow! That was wild. Did I do that myself?"

"I provided no assistance in that maneuver, Gideon."

"Does my body need to be...almost dead to be able to do this?"

"No, but thought-travel will not be accomplished by the human race for another several thousand years. You are only now beginning to scratch the surface of the potential of the right side of your brain."

"Why will it take us so long?" Gideon asked, more interested in the flight than the answer to his question.

"Because you are still so young. Just as an infant must sit before it stands and crawl before it walks, so too does awareness take time to develop."

"Awareness?" asked Gideon.

"Yes, awareness. At this stage of your development your awareness is quite limited. If I could compare your awareness to your physical development, you are just reaching the stage where the infant begins to sit unsupported.

"You only perceive what your five senses submit to your brain."

"What else is there?" Gideon asked, his interest shifting from the planet to the answer.

"How about me?" Zack answered. "I've been by your side like stink on ..., well, never mind the analogy. I've been with you like a loving parent from the moment you were born, yet only now do you see me."

"Why did you hang around if I couldn't see you or hear you? I mean, what good are you if I can't hear your advice?"

Gideon noticed a large bird, unlike any he had seen on earth, soaring over the peak of the highest mountain.

"You could hear me, Gideon. You just didn't know it was me. I'm that little voice in your head that you think is you. Most of the time it is, but there are times when I come through, like your question to Dr. Spiro about the ocean that the iceberg floats in."

"But I never see you," Gideon protested.

"Do you remember two years ago standing on the corner of Hazard Street?" Zack asked. "You were paying no attention to traffic and stepped off the curb into the path of an oncoming truck. An old man with a white beard, tattered clothing and pushing a grocery-cart filled with his worldly possessions jerked you back just in time. Do you remember?"

The realization hit Gideon like a truck plowing through a brick wall. "That was you!" He shrieked in astonishment. "But if I could see you then, why can't I see you all the time?"

"It takes great energy for us to materialize a body and it is exceptionally depleting. Therefore, we only materialize during the direst of emergencies where your body is in peril before completing your life-task."

This information stretched Gideon's awareness to the limit. His mind felt like a balloon that was blown-up to the point of popping, and before it exploded he refocused his attention on Moebius below. The mountain range above which he hovered extended from one end of the kidney-shaped continent to the other. It looked like a ragged brown and white belt made by a child.

"Moebius is a young planet," Zack explained. "The creator has high hopes for it. Come! Let me show you."

Gideon and Zacharaias traversed the planet in what seemed an instant, yet every detail of the earth-sized planet registered on his mind. The twelve oceans running in color from black to sky blue; the ten continents, some flat, barren and sandy brown and others lush, undulating and kaleidoscopic in their range of colors reminded Gideon of earth. The thought travelers saw active volcanos, fierce hurricanes that leveled the vegetation that lay in their path, lightning storms that ignited the forests, and earthquakes that split the skin of Moebius like a sharp knife.

They also saw the peaceful face of the planet; gentle waves lapping white-sand beaches under clear blue skies; lush tropical forests teeming with wildlife very similar to earth's, and huge azure lakes upon which nested all forms of water fowl.

"There are no people on Moebius," Gideon observed.

"It is being prepared," came Zack's cryptic reply. "Come. It is time for you to visit the Gatekeeper."

Chapter Six

As the galaxies sped by, Gideon thought of the similarities between Moebius and Earth. Although he had done little or no traveling, the technological age in which he lived brought the wonders of his home planet to the twenty-five-inch screen in his living room. On those occasions when he was not allowed to watch MTV because his parents were watching NOVA or National Geographic, Gideon forced himself to view the mysteries of his own world.

In the quietness and solitude of his mind Gideon reluctantly admitted that the volcanic eruption of Mt. Kilueha in Hawaii was more spectacular than watching MTV, although both had a place in his life. He was mesmerized by the sight of the Earth's most formidable species standing helplessly by while the inexorable slow-motion flow of lava made a meal of everything in its path.

"Why does the Earth have so many bad things happen? I mean, why does it have earthquakes and volcanic eruptions, hurricanes and tornadoes, lightning and fire?" Gideon's attention was momentarily diverted by a brilliant three-star system that whizzed by just above him. He thought of his asteroid dream the night of the ice storm.

"The Universe is alive, Gideon, just as you are alive," Zack replied. "As your body changes and grows, so does the Earth. You have your breath, the Earth has its atmosphere. You sneeze, the Earth has a hurricane. You cough, it tornadoes. You cry, it rains. You lash out in anger, its volcanoes erupt. You cut yourself, the

Earth quakes. You have your blood, the Earth has its water. Your arteries carry your blood to feed your body, the Earth has its rivers to feed the land. The Earth is infinitely more than a mere orb upon which you happen to reside. It is your living home."

"Why do we pollute it then?" Gideon asked as a red dwarf star exploded into a super nova directly in front of him.

"For the same reason you pollute your own bodies with drugs, alcohol and tobacco," Zack replied. "You are unaware of the sacredness of all things. How can you respect the Earth when you have yet to learn to respect yourselves. Just as the human infant's awareness is such that it will swallow poison if made available, so too is the awareness of your species at the infantile stage. You are learning, however.

"Look! The door to the Land of the Gatekeeper is just ahead."

Floating in the black void, spinning slowly like a merry-go-round, was a red door, a door attached to nothing and apparently opening into nothing.

"Grab the handle and open the door, Gideon," Zack said, gently nudging his companion toward the opening.

"But it's just a door floating in space," Gideon objected.

"And your body is lying at the bottom of Round Pond and you are here. There are many realities. Open the door."

Gideon reached for the golden knob and turned it hesitantly to the right. As the door opened Gideon saw brilliant sunlight on the other side, but none escaped into the darkness in which he stood.

"Go on through, Gideon. There's nothing in the Land of the Gatekeeper that will hurt you. It is a world much like your own where each soul creates its own reality."

"Talk English, will ya, Zack!" Gideon said. "What does 'create your own reality' mean?"

"You must discern that for yourself, but if you remember your mother's words about four billion people and four billion worlds you'll have a leg-up on the answer."

With a gentle yet firm shove, Zack pushed Gideon through the portal then stepped through himself. The Twilight Zone was stuff for three-year-olds compared to this, Gideon thought. In every direction, as far as his eyes could see, was desert sand, but not like any desert he had ever seen on Earth. This desert glimmered like welding sparks, and had he been in his body Gideon would have needed a welder's visor just to keep his eyes open. In his current condition, however, the brightness of the landscape merely heightened his appreciation of its beauty.

"What am I going to learn here?" Gideon complained, sounding like his old self. "There's nothing here but sand. It's beautiful, but I'm fourteen. I'd like a little action."

"Look again," Zack said. He pointed eastward, and sitting on the horizon, in stark contrast to the blue sky, was an immense walled-city. From his vantage point, some twenty miles away, Gideon saw five crystal spires reaching to the angel-hair clouds a thousand feet overhead. The city was laid out in a square with one spire standing sentinel in each corner, while the fifth rose out of the center. As they approached the city, Gideon realized it was surrounded by a fifty-foot gray stone wall, and sitting atop the wall was a glass bubble. It finished the job of enclosing the city that the stone wall began. It looked as though the entire city was climate controlled.

"Why is the city enclosed? There doesn't seem to be any way in," Gideon said as they thought-traveled around the immense metropolis.

"The only way in is through the Gatekeeper," Zack said. "Anyone can leave whenever they choose, but all those wishing to enter must first speak with the Gatekeeper."

"He sounds like a security guard at a bank or something. Does he wear a gun?"

Zack chuckled. "Look! You can see him now, off in the distance. Straight ahead."

Gideon's eyes followed the line of Zack's pointing finger. Two hundred yards ahead, in front of a gleaming gold door as high as the stone wall, stood the Gatekeeper.

"Will the Gatekeeper be able to see us?" Gideon asked.

"The Gatekeeper sees all. Come, let us pay him our respects."

The Gatekeeper was ancient, older even than Zacharaias. His face was so deeply furrowed with the creases of age that were he to lie on his back during a rain-storm they would have held a enough water to quench a thirst. His hair was as white as the down of a gosling. It was drawn tight against his head and tied off in the back to form a pony tail that hung lazily to the center of his back. The old man had bushy eyebrows that came within an ant lip's length of meeting just above the bridge of his long, bulbous nose. Tufts of long white hair stood atop each ear like antennae.

His body was short, lean, and erect and looked as though it still carried much of the power of his youth. But it was his eyes, as it was Zack's eyes, that drew Gideon in. They were as blue and as deep as the lacquer on a new Ferrari, and seemed to see straight into Gideon's soul. Everything about the Gatekeeper proclaimed him to be a 'Wise Old Man.'

"Why does this city have such an old man for a Gate-keeper?" Gideon whispered to Zack, lest the Gatekeeper hear him.

"Anyone could get by him."

"So, you think I'm an old relic, do you, Gideon?" His voice was steady and firm, seemingly uncracked by the weight of life and time.

"Well...You are old," Gideon stammered, "but...I don't know, you're different from all the old people I know."

The Gatekeeper smiled, and the furrows of his brown weathered face narrowed. "How so?" he asked, learning eons ago that a teacher's best tool was a well timed question.

"Where I come from," Gideon began, "old people look like you... sort of. I mean, their bodies look like yours, but somehow theirs seem more tired and bent, as though they were weighed down by some heavy load. You have an old body, but you seem... light."

"Well put. I too have noticed that the aged in your world look old in their bodies," the Gatekeeper said. His eyes twinkled and Gideon noticed the trace of a smile, evident only at the corners of his mouth.

"I don't get you," Gideon said. "And how did you know my name?"

"Ah, you humans are so young and have so much still to learn. Your old people act and feel old, because they place such a premium on youth. They value youth above all else and see old age as a time of loss and burden. They therefore meet those expectations of themselves."

"But what good is being old?" Gideon said, not getting the Gatekeeper's point. "They're forgetful. Some are senile. They've lost their strength. Their kids have to take care of them. They don't look good in bathing suits."

"Enough!" The Gatekeeper put up his hand. "All you say is true, but it need not be true for all time. Your young people

49

must rethink what it means to be old, or their fate will be that of their grandparents. Old age is the most spiritual of all the stages of life. It should be a time for reflection and life-review, for it comes directly before your return to the Creator. It need not be worse than the stage of life you call youth, but it does need to be different. If what you value is running fast and looking good in a bathing suit, then of course old age will weigh you down."

"You still haven't told me how you knew my name."

"I heard Zacharaias speak it on your way here."

"Great hearing!" Gideon said, looking at the long white hairs atop the Gatekeeper's ears.

"You're right. I do have good hearing, but I didn't hear Zacharaias here." The Gatekeeper pointed to his ear. "I heard him here." He pointed to his heart.

Gideon turned at the creak of the golden door, and out walked a boy that looked to be his own age. The boy waved and sent a warm smile toward the Gatekeeper then wandered off into the desert. Gideon looked at the Gatekeeper, and when he turned again to look for the boy, he had disappeared.

"Who was that, and where did he go?" Gideon asked the Gatekeeper.

"The young man's name is Parsifal, and he is off to find another city, another Gatekeeper. He was unable to find his heart here and so will be wandering for many years."

"There are more cities like this, and more men like you?"

"Indeed," said the Gatekeeper. "There are as many cities and Gatekeepers as there are stars in the sky, but not all of us are men. Half our ranks are filled with women."

"But where are the other cities? When we thought-traveled here, we only saw this one. The rest of your world seems to be desert," Gideon said, convinced of his own perceptions.

"That is because you only see with your eyes and not with your heart. Parsifal is off to find his heart, and when he does he will be able to see. He is like you in many ways." The Gatekeeper tugged on his chin and looked up as one often does when trying to catch a thought. "I think I would like to invite you and Zacharaias to sit with me for a spell while I perform my duties. Will you join me?"

Zack looked at Gideon. "Sure," Gideon said, "but what exactly is it you do?"

As though on cue, a young girl who looked as though she had only recently entered the mysteries of womanhood, appeared before the Gatekeeper. She was dark-skinned and well manicured, but her walk and her posture belied her beautiful exterior. The girl shuffled over to the Gatekeeper as though her shadow weighed more than her body.

"Welcome traveler," the Gatekeeper said. "You look as though your journey has been long and arduous. What is it you are in search of?"

She seemed not to see Gideon and Zacharaias for her gaze went beyond them to the fifty-foot golden door. "My name is Tanisha, Gatekeeper, and you are wise to know that my walk upon this land has blistered my feet."

"What is it you are in search of, young woman?"

"I search for a city whose inhabitants treat each other with respect and kindness, a city that knows no hatred, and where all people are looked upon as equals."

"A noble search, Tanisha," the Gatekeeper acknowledged. "A noble search indeed. Might there be more you are looking for?"

"Yes, Gatekeeper. I am looking for a place where a

51

stomach never cries for food, where children are treated with more respect than their parents' cars, and where depression is known only as a dip in the road."

"You are wise to desire such things, Tanisha," the Gatekeeper said, nodding. "But tell me. Could you not find these things in the land from which you came? Tell me of the place you left."

"It is everything my Nirvana is not," Tanisha cried. "There is no fairness. The rich hoard and the poor starve. Parents are children and children have babies. The chain cannot be broken. Could this city, whose gates you guard, be the one I search for?"

The Gatekeeper shook his head sorrowfully. "This city is not the one you search for. If you were not able to find the things you search for in the city you left, you will certainly not find them through this golden gate. You will find everything you left behind, right here."

Tanisha sighed and turned toward the desert. A single tear dropped from her eye and moistened the sand in front of her feet. The young girl continued her resolute march toward a place only she could create. As long as she persevered in the search there was hope of finding what she longed for.

"What kind of city are you the Gatekeeper of?" Gideon asked. He picked up the moistened sand created by the mournful girl's teardrop and threw it at the Gatekeeper.

"What kind of city would you like it to be?" the wise old man asked, catching the sandy missile in his hand. Gideon's reply was cut-off by another traveler. This time it was a middle-aged man, smartly dressed and apparently in good physical condition. His face was as deeply tanned as the Gatekeeper's and Gideon sensed he had been in the desert for a long, long time. He looked vaguely familiar.

"Greetings, Gatekeeper," the man said excitedly. "Do you remember me?"

The Gatekeeper smiled in his knowing way. "Need you ask, Parsifal? You had just turned fourteen when you left through that golden gate thirty-five years ago. What is it you seek?"

"I seek what I refused to see when I left," Parsifal replied. "I went from Gatekeeper to Gatekeeper, each telling me their golden door would admit me to a world that was a carbon-copy of the one I left. If I saw fear and hatred in this city, I would find it in the next. If I thought others got the luck while I got the shaft, that too would I find in every city the Gatekeepers attended.

"My journeys taught me much, Gatekeeper," Parsifal continued. "I seek to enter the gates through which I passed thirty-five years ago."

"And what do you expect to find that you did not find before?" the Gatekeeper asked. "How will my city be different this time?"

"If I expect unfairness, I will find it. If I expect fairness, I will find that also. If it is love that I seek, it is love that I will find. But should I have hatred in my heart, it is hatred that will find me. There will be abundance and there will be scarcity. Abundance for those who seek it and scarcity for those who expect it. All these things were present when I left, but I only saw the unfairness, the hatred and the scarcity. The other Gatekeepers were right in telling me that was all I would find in their cities."

"You have learned well, Parsifal." The Gatekeeper embraced the younger man, who brought back memories of his own journey scores of years earlier. With the embrace the golden door opened and Parsifal stepped through to the home he refused to see as a young man.

Gideon was dumbfounded. "That man left your city no

53

more than fifteen minutes ago as a fourteen-year-old. How can that be?"

"How can it be that you are here and your body is at the bottom of Round Pond?" the Gatekeeper asked in return, echoing the words of Zacharaias a short time earlier. "You humans have so much further to travel. If you decide to return to your body, Gideon, you may want to learn something about Quantum Mechanics. Those who do are beginning to see a different world than the one you see. A new world view is being created."

"Quantum Mechanics? Why would I want to learn about working on engines?" Gideon asked.

The Gatekeeper chuckled. "In a way you are right, Gideon. It is the engine of the Universe, the study of the very smallest of particles."

Zacharaias laid his hand lightly on Gideon's shoulder. "We must be going," he said. "Is there anything you'd care to ask the Gatekeeper before we leave for the land of 'What is Good? What is Bad?'"

Gideon thought for a moment then spoke. "Before I fell through the ice on Round Pond I had a dream of a tug-of-war between white and black circles pulling against a golden center. Could you tell me, Gatekeeper, what this dream means?"

"Your dreams are sent to you by your spirit, Gideon," the Gatekeeper began, "and it is for you to decipher their meaning. I can only tell you how your dream resonates within me and if in doing so it strikes a chord in you then for us the dream has the same meaning. If your dream were mine it might be telling me that there are parts of me that need to be united, parts that seem to be opposite, but if reconciled would be turned to gold. Learn the story of the Prodigal son."

A new traveler appeared, and the Gatekeeper ceased his interpretation of Gideon's dream. "I'm sorry, Gideon, but as you can see, a new traveler demands my attention. Good luck in your travels with Zacharaias, and remember, the way to self-knowledge is through a narrow gate. The path is difficult, and few will choose it. The wide way is easy and many will take it, but it will never lead you to your own truth. I bid you ado."

Chapter Seven

Y ou didn't have much to say," Gideon said as he and Zacharaias sped away from the Land of the Gatekeeper and back through the door through which they entered.

"The visit wasn't for me, Gideon. Millions of years ago a guide, much like myself, first introduced me to the Land of the Gatekeeper. Lessons once learned stay with us always."

"What lessons are those?"

"You speak of luck and of unfairness just as I did as a young man. The lesson of the Gatekeeper is that as long as you believe luck and unfairness determines the course of your life you will find it wherever you go."

As the galaxies sped by, Gideon reflected on his life and how Zack's words seemed to penetrate his mind as easily as an arrow pierces a straw target. He tried to squeeze some meaning from what he heard. "If I believe everything that happens to me is fair and that luck plays no part in my destiny then my life will be perfect?"

"Your life is already perfect, and always has been. You just stopped believing it at an earlier age than most. You came into life for spiritual growth and to assist the creator in creation. If, in your conscious mind, the mind that makes you aware, you move away from the path your soul has chosen to follow, then you will experience events that will hopefully move you back on your path. That is part of my job as your spiritual guardian.

"For example," Zack continued, "many teenagers turn to

alcohol and drugs for a high. Wanting this 'high' is perfectly normal for humans, for unconsciously you all desire the vaguely remembered experience of the reality you find yourself in now. Some of you call it heaven, but it is merely a state of being at peace."

"I didn't remember that experience," Gideon said.

"Consciously you don't remember, but unconsciously you remember everything. Do you remember that iceberg Dr. Spiro used as an example? The visible part is your conscious mind, but the bulk of the iceberg is below the surface, out of view. That part, the submerged part, remembers, and unconsciously your reason for using alcohol and drugs is to regain that spiritual 'high,' that sense of oneness with the cosmos."

"Then why does everyone say it's bad?" Gideon asked.

"Because as humans you are meant to experience life consciously, to make sentient all that lies in the unconscious. This is your evolutionary path. Because you seek a spiritual path unconsciously, the form it takes becomes destructive. Do you know the myth of the Phoenix, Gideon?" Zack asked.

"The only thing I know about the Phoenix," Gideon replied, "is that a city in Arizona is named after it."

"The Phoenix is a bird that appears in many world myths. It is a bird that burns itself on its own altar and perpetually rises from its own ashes. It is one of the early models of the resurrection. Like the Phoenix, the contents of our unconscious perpetually attempt a resurrection through the light of consciousness. If we refuse to become conscious, to become awake, our unconscious will throw us into the fiery furnace in an attempt to resurrect itself. After all, there could never have been a Christian resurrection had there not been a crucifixion."

"So you're saying that sometimes bad things happen to get

us to move away from a place where we're stuck?" Gideon asked.

"Yes. If we don't pay attention to the more subtle signs the messages will get stronger."

"So in a way the bad things that happen to us, or the bad that we do, really aren't bad. Right?"

"There are many levels of meaning," Zack replied. "And a perfect example is to be found in the Diamond Galaxy where we will find the land of 'What is Good? What is Bad.'"

"How do we get there?"

"Take my hand and think 'fast'. I'll do the navigating. If we were in one of your spaceships the journey would take fifteen trillion years, hardly a manageable time frame. This is why thought-travel will be the way you explore the Universes. Are you ready?"

"Ready," Gideon replied. He held his breath as though he were about to jump into a river from a train bridge.

"Those specks of stars you see are about to streak, as a child's fingers will streak a dewy window. Watch as they change color. I thought you might enjoy the light show so I've slowed down our speed."

As Zacharaias and Gideon surpassed the speed of light the Universe became light, and the two began traveling back in time. The trillions upon trillions of nuclear infernos that each star represented turned into highways of colored light, a Universe full of rainbows, beginning and ending in infinity.

"Look ahead and to your left, Gideon," Zack said. "Do you see it?"

Gideon looked as he was instructed and saw an immense black funnel in the middle of one of the red highways.

"What is it?" Gideon asked. "It looks like a tornado."

"It is what your scientists call a Black Hole, a star that has collapsed in on itself and whose gravitational field is so strong, no light can escape it."

"Wow," Gideon said, surprised that he understood what Zack was saying.

"Your scientists are on the verge of discovering that these Black Holes are actually doorways to different Universes."

"Did you say Universes? Like more than one?" Gideon asked. "I thought you said Universes before, but I figured I misheard you."

"They are infinite in number," Zacharaias replied, as though the knowledge of infinite Universes was kids stuff.

Gideon let loose a high-pitched whistle, for to him this was headline news. As he and Zack grew closer to the Black Hole, Gideon noticed other journeyers. To his left he saw a young girl, no more than ten years old, holding hands with her spirit guide, a woman of indeterminate age and dressed in a robe much like Zack's. The little girl was clothed in a hospital gown. Gideon saw the same silver thread attached to her that was attached to his body that lay light years away at the bottom of Round Pond. Her's reached back as far as his eyes could see. He was reminded of his sister, Prudence, and how much he missed her, although he would never admit it. Gideon wondered if she had made it to the fire station yet.

Gideon turned to Zacharaias. "Is that little girl dead?" he asked.

"Not as long as the silver thread remains," Zack replied. "The girl's name is Tarla. She has Leukemia and is in the midst of a crisis. Her doctors are trying to revive her as I speak. Her home planet is Zontar."

"But she's human!" Gideon shrieked. He didn't know if he

could stand many more surprises.

"Indeed," Zack said. "Humans are the God-seed of the Universe. It is through you that the Creator becomes conscious of her creation. That is why it is so important that you become aware of the contents of the unconscious."

"Am I going to remember all of this if I decide to stay alive?"

"You will remember, but not all at once. The lessons you learn on this journey will become available to you as you need them."

"It looks like everyone is getting sucked down a drain," Gideon said, changing his attention back to the Black Hole. "How will we get back out? Everything is going into the funnel, but nothing is coming out."

"Nothing ever escapes out of a Black Hole, with the exception of a particle or two of light," Zacharaias explained. "But each Universe is connected to every other Universe by these Black Holes. They are like entrance and exit doors, worm holes so-to-speak, each opening in only one direction. To get back to this Universe we merely find the exit in that Universe that connects it to this Universe."

"God has a lot of irons in the fire, doesn't he?"

"Yes, she does, Gideon," Zack said, wondering if Gideon caught the change in pronouns when he referred to God.

"Why do you keep calling God a 'she?'" Gideon asked.

"Why do you keep calling God a 'he?'" Zack asked in return.

"Because I was taught God is a man."

"But it says in your Bible that you were created in the image of the Creator. Your interpretation, Gideon, would exclude half the human race from that image."

"Yeah, but how can we or God be both male and female?" Gideon asked, sure Zack was playing with his mind.

"Your bodies can't, but the energies within you can. Whether you know it or not, you learned much at Dr. Spiro's office. Do you remember the picture hanging in the hallway of his home, the one that you referred to as two fishes eating each other's tail?"

"Yes," Gideon answered. "Susan called it the symbol of the Tao, the Way."

"That's correct, Gideon. Some refer to those two fishes of yours, the black and the white, as yin and yang, male and female."

"And each fish has an eye the color of its opposite's body," Gideon joined in.

"Very good," Zack said. "Each fish has its opposite's energy located at its very center, and, in this way each human being carries both aspects of the Creator despite the sex of the carrier."

"You're saying I'm part girl inside," Gideon asked in disbelief. He looked around to see if anyone was within ear-shot.

"How could you ever fully represent the Creator if you weren't? How could you ever become what you potentially could be if both aspects of the creator were not forever present within you? Male and female still have much to learn from each other."

"No one will ever believe this back home," Gideon said.

"Many already do, but it will be some time before you remember this teaching, if you decide to return to your body."

"So... Jenny Bloom is part man, and I'm part woman," Gideon mused. "Wild, Zack. Just wild."

"Your race is still many generations away from balancing their energies, but, when you do, the gate to that paradise you think you lost will be refound."

"Paradise isn't in heaven?"

"The heavens are mostly empty space," Zack answered, as they approached the outer rim of the Black Hole. "We've traveled billions of light years and through millions of galaxies. Have you seen a heaven? Paradise has always been right in front of your noses, but you were too blind to see it. For part of the soul to incarnate... ."

"Incarnate?" Gideon asked.

"For part of the soul to be in a body, and therefore in space and time, is its greatest means of learning. In fact, it is the only way."

"Why do you say part of the soul incarnates?" Gideon asked. "I always thought the soul was somewhere inside of us, like in our chest or something."

"The soul is no puny thing, Gideon. The body resides in the soul, not the other way around. It provides the vehicle through which the soul learns."

"You mean becomes conscious?" Gideon asked.

"Now you're getting the idea. Come. It is time to enter the Land of What is Good? What is Bad?"

The center of the Black Hole, the door through which they were to pass, was vast. Gideon estimated its diameter to be equal to that of the Earth's, but the bottom of the funnel, the part that opened to the other Universe, was just wide enough to accommodate two people. It reminded Gideon of a water whirlpool going down a dish drain, wide at the top, but very small at the bottom.

Gideon and Zacharaias entered the Black Hole directly behind the little girl, Tarla, and her guide. "Is it possible for me to talk to any of the other guides and their..." Gideon thought for a moment, his finger absently scratching his temple. "What are we called when we're not in our bodies?" he asked.

"Yes, it is possible for you to speak with whomever you wish. You are called a spirit when you are not in your body. I am a spirit guide. That is to say, I am the guide of a spirit, namely you."

Gideon looked at Tarla, who flashed a toothy smile in return. At ten her teeth were closer to their adult size than was the rest of her body. She was thin and most of her blond hair was gone as a result of her chemotherapy. Gideon wanted to approach her, and, as though reading his mind, Tarla motioned him to join her.

"Hi," she said. "Zondata tells me your name is Gideon, and you are from the planet Earth."

"And you're from Zontar. Zacharaias says your name is Tarla."

"Yes," the young girl said, wishing she had remembered to wear her head bandanna before drifting toward death. "I don't usually look like this. I've been sick."

"I know," Gideon said. "Zack told me. You're very pretty, and your hair will grow back."

"Thank you, you're very kind," Tarla said, a furrow creasing her brow. "Until I nearly died I didn't know that there were Samans on other planets. Zondata, my guide, says we are everywhere and that we are God's seed."

It took Gideon a moment to realize what Samans were. "We're called humans on Earth, and I have a sister about your age. You remind me of her, except she wasn't sick. She was a pain in the neck, but I guess I was a bigger pain. Do you have any brothers or sisters?"

"I have two brothers," Tarla answered. "Zimec and Rondar. Both are older than me. Rondar is fourteen, and Zimec is eighteen.

Rondar never liked me much until I got Leukemia. He was always complaining that life was unfair, that Zimec was better looking, that Zimec was smarter and stronger. Rondar complained about everything. He took his anger at the world and his jealousy of Zimec out on me. I think he was really angry at himself."

"Sounds familiar," Gideon said, guilt dripping from his voice like honey from a bear-clawed hive.

"Anyway, when I got Leukemia, Rondar began to change. It was almost as if I was supposed to get Leukemia just to wake up Rondar. It was my gift to him. At least that's what Zondata says."

"Have you decided to go back to your body yet?" Gideon asked, looking at her silver thread.

"Not yet. This is like a vacation. I feel so good in my spirit form, and I know if I go back to my body there will be more pain and suffering. Zondata is showing me things that will help me if I decide to return."

"I haven't decided either, but I'm beginning to get the feeling that there is much more for me to do back on Earth."

"Me too," Tarla agreed, "and I really miss my parents. They've been wonderful and have learned a lot about themselves from my illness. Zondata says that sometimes an old soul incarnates into a weak body just to provide lessons and growth opportunities for familiar souls that we love. She says I'm an old soul. An old soul is not really old, because all souls were created at the same time. An old soul, Zondata says, is a wise soul, one that learns faster. It would be pretty dull if we were all the same."

"I don't know if I'm an old soul or not," Gideon said. "But I sure don't feel like one. I was a real complainer and sounded much like your brother, Rondar. How did your illness change him?"

"Well, it's hard to continue thinking life is unfair when you are healthy and strong and your little sister is battling for her life with Leukemia. He couldn't be the 'poor me' kid anymore once I got Leukemia. It sort of stinks for me, but when you think about it, it was good for Rondar."

"It's funny how a bad thing can have some good in it," Gideon said, realizing for the first time what Simon meant about seeing manure as crap or fertilizer. He became excited about his impending visit to the Land of What is Good? What is Bad?

Their descent through the Black Hole made the Cyclone at Riverside park in Massachusetts seem as tame as an old house dog. They dropped as though sucked from below by an industrial-strength vacuum cleaner while spinning around the circumference of the funnel with a centrifugal force so strong they couldn't close their eyes. As the funnel's circumference grew smaller their bodies began to stretch like so many pieces of salt water taffy, until they finally reached the end and were spit out into the adjoining Universe like pieces of over-chewed bubble gum. They were scattered in all directions, millions of them.

Gideon was more impressed with the ride through the Black Hole, but wondered about the numbers of fellow travelers. "Why are there so many spirits going to the Diamond Universe?" Gideon asked Zack.

"No more are going to the Diamond Universe than to any other," Zack replied. "Each Universe offers its own teachings, and each guide determines which Universe would be the most appropriate for each lesson. I have friends who chose the Land of What is Good? What is Bad? in your Universe rather than the Diamond Universe."

"Why did you choose the Diamond Universe for me?" Gideon asked, noticing for the first time that some spirits had the silver thread attached and some didn't.

"For the same reason you go to Burger King sometimes instead of McDonald's. For a change of pace. You get the same beef, but the fixins' are different. You'll find the same lessons in the Diamond Universe as in any other, but the fixins' are different.

"You better say good-bye to Tarla," Zack said. "We're going in different directions, and you won't be seeing her again until you leave your body without the silver thread."

Gideon took Tarla's tiny hand and wished her luck. She motioned him to bend down and she kissed him on his cheek, much like Prudence used to do when she was smaller. With no more than a thought she and Zondata were gone, off to a place that Tarla needed to be.

Chapter Eight

The Diamond Universe was much like Gideon's own, but like any twin there were many subtle differences. It occurred to Gideon that he knew the name of the Diamond Universe, but didn't know the name of his own, so he asked his guide.

"They all belong to you," Zack replied.

"Maybe they all belong to me, but I live in another Universe. What's the name of the Universe in which I live?"

Zack smiled. "You live in them all, Gideon, but if you mean the one where you lie at the bottom of Round Pond it is called the Gold Universe."

A wave of goose bumps crawled across Gideon's ethereal flesh as his mind struggled with the information he had just received. It was more startling than any of the other surprises Zack had pulled from his magician's hat. "Are you telling me I'm not the only me?" Flies would have had easy access to Gideon's mouth had there been any to take advantage of its gaping yaw.

"There are as many Gideons as there are Universes," Zack chuckled, delighted in the effect his disclosure created.

"And I suppose there are an infinite number of Universes."

Zack smiled again and nodded. "Each one of you in some way influences the rest. There are an infinite number of possibilities that your life could have lived out and each of these actualizes in another Universe."

The soul is no puny thing, Gideon remembered Zack saying. "Is that why you said I'm only part of my soul?" he asked.

"Very good, Gideon. And all the other Gideons make up the rest. Your soul lives out all of life's possibilities. This is why I said the soul in no puny thing," Zack said after having read Gideon's mind. "Come! We need not concern ourselves with this right now, but if you will look to your left at approximately nine o'clock you will see a most familiar sight."

Their speed was slow enough so the heavenly bodies held their form and color. Gideon looked as he was directed and exactly where Zack had pointed was the planet Earth and its single moon.

"I'm going to wake up and all of this is going to be a dream," Gideon said. "Is that what I think it is?" Gideon pointed to the planet suspended like a jewel in front of him.

"Each Universe is an image of every other. What differs is the soul activity that takes place within each. What you see is Earth, but Earth as it was in the year 520 BC. The Land of What is Good? What is Bad? will be found in China of that year."

"And I'll bet there's a lesson to be learned there," Gideon said sarcastically. His tone and words were said out of habit, but his feeling of excitement was new.

"There are lessons in everything," Zack answered. "There are no such things as coincidences. Every event has meaning if your eyes are open to see and your ears ready to hear. We will be observers in the Land of What is Good? What is Bad? The people will not be able to see us. It will be like watching a movie except we'll be interwoven into the scene like invisible thread."

Before heading for their specific destination Zacharaias took Gideon on a tour of the Earth as it had been 2500 years earlier. The layout of the planet was much as it is today, with twenty-five centuries being nothing more than a single cosmic breath in terms of geological change.

"Notice anything different?" Zack asked, as they thought-traveled from continent to continent.

"If I had to sum it up," Gideon said, scratching his chin, and marveling at his heightened ability to think, "it would have to be the effect 2500 years of civilization had on the planet."

"And what does that look like?"

"The air is as clear as Crystal Pepsi, even on the east coast of North America. And the forests look so different."

"How do you mean different?" Zack asked, prodding his pupil to answer his own questions.

"Older," Gideon answered. "They're so much bigger and taller than the big ones the timber industry cuts down today. They almost seem wise, as though they've actually absorbed the history they've lived through. Looking at them reminds me of the Gatekeeper, but they're only trees, aren't they?"

Zack smiled at the blossoming wisdom his charge was exhibiting.

"What are you smiling at?" Gideon asked.

"Oh, nothing," Zack replied, regaining his composure. "Describe to me what you see."
Zack was teaching by asking questions, for he knew Gideon already had the answers deep within him.

"I see paradise," Gideon said. "Is this what you meant when you said, 'Paradise is in front of our noses, but we're too blind to see it?'"

Zack remained still, and in his stillness answered Gideon's question.

"Does it seem to you that I'm getting smarter?" Gideon asked. "I mean... I don't think I'd be able to answer your questions before I went to the bottom of Round Pond. I always thought I was stupid."

"In your Spirit-form you have no hang-ups, as you call them. Your energy flows freely, and you are able to tap into your ancient wisdom. After all, you were there at the beginning with the Creator. This increase in wisdom happens gradually, of course, but I can see that even in the eye-blink of time we've been together, you have begun to tap into your greater source."

"I thought it was something like that," Gideon lied.

"I see you are also clinging to some of your old ways, my young friend," Zack said, referring to the lie. "No matter. This is all quite natural."

Gideon would have turned red had he been in his physical body. Being caught in a lie was always humiliating for him, and he had lied often.

"Is there an Earth somewhere that is in the future?" Gideon asked. "It would be cool to have my own crystal ball."

"You pick the year, and we'll take a side trip after the lesson of the Land of What is Good? What is Bad?"

Gideon and Zacharaias finished their Earth tour of the year 520 BC and headed for central China and the farm of Wu Li. His was one of several small farms in a fertile river-valley that Wu Li's family had worked for twenty generations. The emperor allowed them enough food to support themselves and enough profit for Wu Li to purchase the first horse his family ever owned. At forty years of age, Wu Li was growing old, for in the year 520 BC the average life span rarely exceeded forty-five years. Likewise his horse, a gray mare in her twentieth year, was also growing old. Other than his eighteen-year-old son, who was his only living heir, the gray mare was Wu Li's most prized possession. His wife died the year before, and in those days wives were possessions.

Zack explained all of this to Gideon as they approached

70

Wu Li's farm under the glow of a full moon. Despite the moon's radiance the stars glistened brighter than the sun after leaving the darkness of a noon matinee. His heart ached at the recognition that his parents' generation and the few preceding it succeeded in spewing enough poison into the atmosphere to change the heavens from the brilliance of a 100-watt bulb to that of a 15-watt night-light. Zacharaias drew him out of his thoughts by directing his attention to a small corral where Wu Li kept his beloved gray mare.

The corral was larger than necessary for one old horse, but Wu Li's love for the mare overrode the more practical consider-ations of maintaining a lone horse on the Emperor's land. The more land devoted to keeping the horse, the less land available for farming. When Wu Li built the corral large enough for ten horses his neighbors told him it was a bad thing to devote so much land to a single horse. Wu Li responded by saying, "Who knows what is good and what is bad?"

The fencing of the corral was weathered and weak. Time and its allies, the weather, the sun and the insects, joined forces to soften the once-strong wood planking. Gideon noticed Wu Li's horse scratching its withers against a single creaking cross-beam that snapped under the pressure. The bony old mare stood there at first, not knowing what to do with her newly found freedom. Once the taller grasses outside her enclosure caught her attention however, she was quick to leave the familiar confinement of her corral.

"Isn't there anything we can do, Zack?" Gideon asked, surprised at his willingness to help.

"We are here to observe and to learn. There is nothing we can do."

Wu Li woke with the morning's light and was quick to

71

discover his loss. To Gideon's surprise he seemed unconcerned. By mid-day word of Wu Li's great loss spread throughout the valley, and his neighbor came offering his condolences. Chou Lo was ten years younger than the graying Wu Li and decades less wise, for indeed, all in the valley considered Wu Li a sage.

"I've come to offer my condolences, Wu Li," Chou Lo said. "Such a terrible loss. Just terrible."

Wu Li continued working his field in silence, thinking about Chou Lo's words before he spoke. "Who knows what is good and what is bad, Chou Lo? Surely I do not."

Chou Lo scratched his head. Certainly, he thought, Wu Li must be losing his mind, for everyone knows that the loss of a horse is a bad thing. He said good-bye and walked the mile back to his farm.

Wu Li was grateful to have his strong son by his side, for without the old gray mare he would not have been able to complete the day's work alone. He might have been able to in his younger days, but certainly not now. The hard day's work was better than any modern-day sleeping pill, and that night Wu Li and his son slept more soundly than ever before.

As Wu Li rose the next morning from his bamboo mat he heard strange noises coming from the recently vacated corral. He shook his son awake and out they went to investigate. Any other man would have trumpeted Wu Li's discovery throughout the valley. His son was not surprised at his father's reaction upon discovering the return of his beloved mare, along with nine wild young horses.

"They must have followed the old mare home, Father," the son said excitedly. "What good fortune."

Wu Li turned slowly to his beaming son. "Who knows

what is good and what is bad? Repair the corral, my son. There is much work to be done."

Again word spread quickly through the fertile valley, this time of Wu Li's exceptionally good luck. Surely the Gods were pleased with Wu Li, they thought, for only the gods could have bestowed such a boon.

The new horses were useless however, until they were broken and trained. To Wu Li's son fell this most difficult task, a chore he had no familiarity with. However, having great common sense, inherited from his father, he chose the smallest of the herd of nine to train first. But even a small horse is far stronger than a big man. In no time Wu Li's son was thrown against the corral fence and landed with such force that his right arm snapped on impact. This was a disaster, for Wu Li would be sorely pressed to keep up the farm until his son's recovery, a fact not unknown by his neighbor, Chou Lo.

As usual, when such events occur, word spread like burning prairie grass of the disaster that befell poor Wu Li. His neighbor Chou Lo once again came bearing condolences.

"Excuse me for being so bold, Wu Li," Chou Lo began, "but this is most horrendous. Yes, most horrendous indeed. You are old, and now you have no help with the farm. If you cannot keep up your quota, the Emperor's tax collector will throw you to the dogs. Yes. This is very bad, very bad indeed."

Wu Li smiled, and his eyes twinkled knowingly. "Chou Lo," he said, "I have told you this truth before, yet you insist upon seeing everything as good or bad. I will tell you again that it is all mixed together. Who knows what is good and what is bad?"

Chou Lo shook his head and looked at his neighbor Wu Li as though his brains just exited his body through his ears. "If you need help," he said, "I can spare you my number-three son. You are my friend even though I think you are crazy sometimes."

"Thank you, Chou Lo. You are a good friend. I will call on number three son if I can no longer do for myself. You must excuse me now, for there is much work to be done by this old man."

Chou Lo began his trek home, wondering how there could be any good in the broken arm of Wu Li's son. The answer came the next day. While Wu Li with his two arms and old body, and his son with his one arm and young body were tending the fields they spied in the distance a cloud of dust. Slowly, at the pace of a walking man, the cloud of dust approached the two laborers. By the time the cloud was within half a mile of Wu Li and his son, they knew it was the Emperor's army on the march. They also knew the army was looking for conscripts to fill its depleted ranks.

A captain of the guard rode up to them on a black steed, twice the size of the old gray mare. He towered above Wu Li and his son while his mount stomped its feet and snorted his disdain. "In the name of our glorious emperor you are commanded forthwith to present your sons for service in the army of the realm." With a disgusted look the captain eyed the old man and his crippled son.

"I have only one son," Wu Li said, "and he stands here by my side."

"The army has no use for a one-armed man," the captain said, spitting at the feet of Wu Li and turning his attention to the corral and the ten horses. "In your son's stead the army will take your herd of horses. I will send my men to gather them. Good day."

As the surly captain was about to ride off he hesitated, remembering tales of a sage that had nine young horses and one old grey mare. Knowing that life in battle was at best tenuous he turned back to the old farmer. "I have a question for you, old man, and if you can answer it to my satisfaction you may keep your old nag."

Wu Li bowed gracefully before the captain who asked, "before I go into battle with my enemies I wish you to teach me about heaven and hell."

Wu Li looked up at the captain and spit on the ground. "How dare you of all people ask me to teach you about heaven and hell. You are a filthy bully, with blood on your sword. You stink. You make me want to retch on the ground from the smell of you. I, teach you of heaven and hell? Why, I doubt that I could teach a lout like you anything. Now get your body out of my sight!"

The captain was stunned that any man would speak to him in such a fashion, let alone such a small and insignificant peasant. His fury rose to a pitch beyond his control. He was speechless with rage and drew his bloody sword and raised it above his head in preparation to slay the wise old farmer.

As his arms began their descent Wu Li looked up and said softly, "That's hell."

The sword ceased its downward arch as the captain heard and then understood Wu Li's meaning. He was overwhelmed at the sacrifice Wu Li was willing to make to show him the meaning of hell and his heart filled with compassion and gratitude. He was finally at peace.

"And that is heaven," Wu Li said, finishing the teaching.

The old gray mare was left in the corral and Wu Li smiled as the captain sped back to his men, who within a fortnight, would all be killed in a bloody battle. "Who knows what is good and what is bad?" Wu Li said as the captain disappeared over the nearest hill.

* * *

"Do you remember the morning after the ice storm?" Zack asked as he and Gideon whisked around the Earth of 520 BC one last time.

"Yes," Gideon replied. "It seems if I put my attention to it I can remember everything that ever happened to me."

"You were complaining to Simon how lucky he was and how unfair life was to you. Do you remember?"

"Yes. Simon told me I always see the dark side of things then used the ice storm as an example of how one event, the ice storm, could be both bad and good. He said he almost got killed driving home in it the night before, but that in the light of day it transformed into a thing of great beauty."

"Sometimes," Zack said, "the dark side or the light side of an event chooses not to show its face for many years, and only by looking back in retrospect can one see the opposite aspect. You can be sure, however, that if you pay attention and allow it, the good will always rise out of the ashes of the bad."

"When does the bad rise out of the good?" Gideon asked.

"When the good does nothing more than inflate you, or to use your language, pump you up, then the good will turn on you, for you misused it. Everything that happens to you in life, Gideon, happens to assist you in your spiritual growth, becoming conscious."

"You mean making more of that iceberg visible above the surface of the water?"

"Exactly. Now, enough of school for the moment. Would you like to see one of the Earths of your future?"

"What do you mean, 'one of the Earths?'" Gideon asked.

"Just as your soul desires to live out all of life's possibilities, so does the Creator desire to live out all possibilities of each Universe." Zack noticed a puzzled look on Gideon's face. "For instance, there is an Earth where the Nazis won World War II. There is an Earth where Jesus was not crucified, but died the natural death of old age. Christianity developed very differently in that world. The possibilities, as you might have guessed, are endless. The Creator is perfect in that all possibilities are lived out."

"How about showing me the Earth fifty years from now?" Gideon asked.

"Which one?" Zack asked, laughing.

"How about the one where I didn't fall through the ice of Round Pond and went on this tour."

"Hold on then and I'll have you there in a thought."

Zacharaias was right, for no sooner had Gideon thought of the Earth fifty years in the future than it appeared before him, but from the vantage point of the moon. The Earth looked as magnificent as it did when Buzz Aldrin, the Apollo 11 astronaut, took his famous picture of Earth rising over the moon's horizon back in July of 1969.

"When seen from this distance," Zack said, "the Earth looks like an oasis in the vast void of space. You can see no national boundaries that have divided mankind for centuries. From here the Earth is One. Let us go closer and see what this version of the future has to offer."

It leaped out at him like a soundly hit baseball in a 3-D movie. There was little or no human activity taking place on the daytime side of the planet. "Where is everybody?" he asked.

"In this version of the future, humans took no action to eliminate hydroflurocarbons..."

77

"Hydro what?" Gideon asked.

"Hydroflurocarbons. That's the chemical agent in aerosol cans that poked a big hole in the ozone layer of your atmosphere. There are several versions of the Earth where hydroflurocarbons were never used, for humans never employed chemicals without a thorough environmental-impact study. In this rendition you see the effect of environmental disregard. The ozone is so depleted here that it became fatal to be out in the sun without highly specialized and expensive protection."

"So human beings have to stay indoors forever in this future?" Gideon asked.

"No. They adapted as they always do in a crisis. They sleep during the day and live their waking lives at night."

"What about the animals?"

"Many species died off, the rest adapted. Insects, of course, mutated quickly and became more pesky than ever."

"Gross," Gideon said, envisioning a world infested with rat-sized cockroaches and mosquitos as big as sparrows. "How will humans change if they can't be out in the sunlight?"

"Well, the evolution of this specific point in time can, of course, go off in infinite directions. But, if this branch fails to heed the signs its environment presents then they will eventually develop eyes much like an owl's. They will be blinded by sunlight and be driven underground by their increasingly poisoned atmosphere. They will filter their oxygen through miles of Earth to their underground burrows. While they are underground the Earth will heal itself, but by then life in the sun will merely be seen as a childish myth."

"You mean the Earth will turn into a paradise again?" Gideon asked.

78

"Yes, but by that time humans will no longer be able to adapt to living aboveground. Their machines will continue to harvest crops grown on the surface, but they will remain in the bowels of the Earth and live their lives much like moles. All Universes are ripe with possibilities, and the human species is the only one in all of creation that has been given the freedom of choosing its own evolution. In this case the Earth had no choice but to drive humans underground."

"How can the Earth have a choice?" Gideon asked, forgetting his earlier discussion with Zack about the living Earth. "Isn't the Earth just a thing?"

"How quickly you have forgotten, Gideon. The Earth is as alive as you and I. Our lives and the Earth's take different forms, but each is alive. The Earth, as a creation of the Creator, has chosen to live the creative life of a host. Its primary conscious function is to provide a home and sustain the life it has created. You can hardly argue that everything on the Earth was born of the Earth."

"Yeah, but that doesn't mean it's alive and can think," Gideon said, being unable to stretch his mind as much as Zack was asking him to.

"It doesn't, eh?" Zack asked, arching his white eyebrows. "I'm going to give you the privilege of watching what your computers have only vaguely imagined. You are going to see one billion years of the life of the entity that loves you as much as your own mother. You are about to see the birth, the growing pains, and the constant evolution of your Mother Earth condensed into the span of one half of one hour. Stand back and behold....**THE EARTH.**

Chapter Nine

To speed the Earth's birth and evolution into the span of a mere thirty minutes was a feat that no humanly-built computer could ever hope to dupli- cate, at least not the way Gideon was about to see it. He hung suspended in the blackness that filled the gap between the moon and Earth, while his guide displayed before him the unimaginable power, splendor, and beauty that is the Earth. He watched as spiraling gases condensed to form a red hot orb tens of thousands of miles in circumference. He watched as the orb cooled from the surface inward forming a molten core that could only release its constantly building pressure through vents to the surface called volcanos.

The early Earth was dynamic and active, much like a toddler, changing constantly and exhibiting a ferocious temper. Gideon watched as the Earth took its first breath, forming an atmosphere that could support its immanent offspring. He saw the rains like he had never seen rain before, enough rain to fill several oceans and seas to a depth of five miles. The monsoons of the Far East were a mere foggy mist in comparison. It was as though the Earth itself was preparing to give birth.

Before Gideon's eyes the surface changed from red to brown to green, while the oceans took on several hues of blue. He watched as the one land mass the scientists called Pangaia split apart and came together then split apart again. He saw India sail into and under the Asian coast, and, in a cataclysmic birthing process, the Himalayas appeared. He watched the Ice Ages come and go and Gideon thought of his own breathing. The American Southwest, once the bottom of a vast ocean, was thrust five thousand feet above sea-level to unite what is now the North American Continent. The process was dynamic and ever-changing, and, had it taken place one thousandth of one percent closer or farther from the sun, the Earth would never have been able to sustain life.

"You can look at it as a cosmic coincidence if you like," Zack said, "but the Earth knew exactly where to be born in order to fulfill its function. It is intelligent, Gideon, and deserves our respect and love for all it has done and continues to do for us."

"That was wild, Zack. The Earth is perpetually moving and changing, just like us. It has more faces than we do. Thanks for showing me such a spectacular process that I had taken so much for granted."

"You are most welcome, my friend. Come, we are off to visit with the Tree Clingers."

"What's so special about the Tree Clingers?" Gideon asked. He scratched his nose and wondered why it itched with no real body to support it.

"They are special in their ignorance of their potential. Their fear has forced them to choose safety rather than the life fully-lived. You will see in a moment. Since you are ready to be your own thought-pilot you may lead the way."

"How do I get us there?"

"All you need to do is think of being in the Land of the Tree Clingers and you will be there. Nothing else is necessary."

"Okay," Gideon said. "Here goes." He closed his eyes, although this was not necessary, thought of the Land of the Tree Clingers, although he didn't know who or where they were, and then opened his eyes. Zacharaias was still by his side smiling

81

broadly while he and Gideon stood in the middle of what appeared to be a tropical rain forest.

"This is too weird," Gideon said. "I think I like it better when we take a little time to get to where we're going. It seems more real."

Zack took Gideon by the hand. "Come," he said. "Let us explore a bit." They set off on a walking tour of the forest that was extraordinarily lush in both vegetation and wildlife. At first glance the flora and fauna appeared much like the varieties found on Earth, but there was one major difference.

"Do you notice anything odd about what you see, Gideon?" Zack asked, unable to control his incessant urge to teach.

Gideon thought for a moment and then noticed a large snake, similar in every way to an Earthly python, grazing on thick green blades of jungle-grass. He saw what looked like a leopard lounging in the lower branches of a tree, feasting on broad dark-green leaves.

"I thought snakes and leopards eat meat?" Gideon said, sure of himself on this one.

"On Earth they do," Zack replied. "Look! Over to your left."

Gideon turned as directed and saw a lion, and what appeared to be a lamb, drinking side by side at a small forest stream.

"Why isn't the lamb afraid of the lion?" Gideon asked.

"Because in the Land of the Tree Clingers there are no carnivores, no meat eaters. The lamb drinks beside the lion for she knows she is not part of the lion's food chain. The lamb has no fear."

"But if there are no meat eaters there are no predators. Why isn't the Land of the Tree Clingers overrun with animals? With no natural enemies how is each species' population kept in check?" Gideon remembered his studies of the animal kingdom and that the food chains kept each species' population from exploding. By rights he and Zack should be waist deep in snakes and rats and all the other animals that breed in great numbers.

"Here the animals keep their numbers down through a less active and less bountiful reproductive system. For instance, that snake you saw eating grass normally lays 30-50 eggs a year on the Earth. But here, because there are no natural predators the female mates once every five years and lays only one egg.

"The Land of the Tree Clingers is a paradise for all but one species," Zack said, and then awaited the question he knew would come.

Gideon, growing in wisdom in his spirit form, surprised his guide. "That species would be the Tree Clingers, right?"

"Very good, Gideon."

"Where are they? I can't see up into the trees because the foliage is so dense. And now that I think of it, I haven't seen any birds here."

"There is only one winged species here, and, if you look closely, you can see their droppings under every large tree."

Gideon looked at the base of a tree so large that two Mack trucks could drive through it side by side if a tunnel were carved for them to do so. At the bottom of the tree, spread out over a circular area the diameter of which Gideon estimated to be at least three hundred feet, were thousands of large greenish brown Tree Clinger droppings in various conditions of decay. The vegetation within the circle was more lush and verdant than anywhere else.

"Potent fertilizer," Gideon joked, "but I'd hate to have one fall on me. They're pretty big. The Tree Clingers must be huge birds."

"The rest of the wildlife are most appreciative of the Tree Clingers for their droppings, although they've never set eyes on them. Let's go up and pay them a visit."

Gideon and Zack materialized at the top of the forest canopy, and still Gideon could not see the Tree Clingers.

"Where are they?" he asked. "They must be about the size of a human to produce such big droppings, but I can't see them anywhere. I can't see them from the forest floor, and I can't see them from the forest canopy."

"Remember, Gideon, the Tree Clingers are the most fearful species in the Universe, and what they fear the most is the unknown. We must descend through the top layer of the canopy to find the Tree Clingers."

As they descended at the speed of a falling snow flake the Tree Clingers appeared before them. There were thousands. The jungle canopy rose three hundred feet above the jungle floor and the entire world of the Tree Clingers took place between one hundred feet and two hundred feet, no higher, no lower. In that middle one hundred feet they arranged themselves in the shape of a pyramid, a single Tree Clinger at the two-hundred- foot boundary and at least one hundred of them at the lower one-hundred-foot boundary. All the other Tree Clingers were arranged in descending numbers as one ascended the tree, and all trees were laid out in the same pyramid form.

This hierarchal arrangement was odd enough, but nothing in comparison to what the Tree Clingers looked like. They were human in every respect but two. Their human legs tapered down to the ankle, and then, expecting to see human feet, Gideon saw bird's feet large enough to wrap around the thickest tree branch.

Growing from the middle of their shoulder blades was a pair of tri-fold white wings, much like that of a bat. A fine white skin covered the thin but strong wing bones that were tucked tightly against their backs. Gideon estimated that if they were fully expanded they would span twenty feet. Their arms and hands were human.

"Wow, I'd give anything for a set of wings like those. Do they only fly at night?" Gideon asked. "I don't see any of them in the air."

"Why don't you ask them?" Zack replied.

"You mean they can see us and hear us?"

"As plainly as you can see and hear them."

Gideon went to the branch upon which stood the top Tree Clinger. "Uh... excuse me Sir...could I speak with you? My name is Gideon McGee."

"My, oh my," the top Tree Clinger moaned in a chirpy kind of voice. "More visitors. You come and you go, you come and you go, and we never remember what it was you came for or what you had to say to us. We have wonderful memories for everything else, but we can't retain any memory of your visits. You say your name is Gideon?"

"Yes, and this is my guide, Zacharaias."

The top Tree Clinger tore a broad leaf from the branch and began munching. Gideon noticed that the branch immediately sprouted a new bud from which a replacement leaf began to grow. The Tree Clinger burped and introduced himself.

"I am Jester, King of this particular tree, dispenser of justice and carrier of the Lore of this tribe, which happens to be the same lore as every other tree tribe." King Jester reached for another leaf and offered it to his guests. His offer being refused, he ate it himself then broke wind.

Gideon laughed. "Do you eat anything else beside these leaves?" he asked, unable to imagine a more boring diet.

This time King Jester manufactured a belch that no two Sumo wrestlers burping together could have matched. Gideon was impressed. It must be all that fiber, he thought.

"Eat anything else?" King Jester bellowed indignantly. "There is nothing else to eat. Look around you. Do you see anything other than these leaves?"

"Not here, but there are many varieties of vegetation down below," Gideon replied.

"There is nothing but broad leaves all the way down to the lowliest dung-covered Tree Clingers. I challenge you to produce any other green thing between here and there."

"You're right, King Jester," Gideon said. "Between you and the lowliest one-hundred there is nothing but green broad-leaves, but I noticed one hundred feet above you the top of your tree is lush with berries and flowers. Having been on the ground I can assure you that there's a world of delicacies down there as well."

"You are either crazy or sent by the devil herself. Our first commandment as Tree Clingers is 'Thou shalt not trespass above two hundred feet'. Our second commandment as Tree Clingers is 'Thou shalt not trespass below one hundred feet'. These are the laws of our book."

"Why don't you just fly to the top of the tree and see for yourself?" Gideon suggested.

"We have everything we need here. Tree Clingers have never gone hungry, as you can see." King Jester proudly patted his protruding belly. Gideon was reminded of his Algebra teacher Mr. Numer. "And what is this 'fly' you speak of?"

"You know," Gideon said, flapping his arms, "Fly. Spread

your wings and soar into the air. Fly!"

It occurred to King Jester that Gideon might be referring to the curse, the hideous growths that grew out of the backs of all Tree Clingers. "You're not talking about these monstrosities, are you?" King Jester asked, pointing disdainfully to the wings on his back.

Gideon turned to Zacharaias who merely shrugged his shoulders. "You're doing fine, Gideon. Continue."

"Those glorious appendages you refer to as monstrosities are called wings. They can take you places you've never imagined. You can soar into the wind and dance among the clouds. Is there not a one of you that has ever flown?" Gideon asked.

As carrier of the lore of the Tree Clingers, King Jester reached far back into his conscious mind, which was not far at all, before answering. "There is something," King Jester said softly, his chirp barely registering on Gideon's ears. "Before our lore was written in bark, legend has it that one Tree Clinger, his name long forgotten, climbed to the topmost branch of the tree and never returned. For all I know his bones may be bleaching in the sun, entwined in the highest branches of this tree."

"I saw no bones at the top of your tree. Did you, Zack?"

"I can assure you, King Jester," Zack said. "There are no bones bleaching in the sun at the top of this tree."

Gideon thought of another tack to take in enlightening King Jester. "Why did God give you hands?" he asked.

"To hold our daily leaves, to assist our young. There are many uses for hands as you well know, having a pair of your own."

"Why do you have eyes?"

"To see."

"Why do you have ears?"

87

"To hear."

"Why do you have teeth?"

"To grind our daily leaves."

"Is there any part of your body, other than your wings, that has no purpose?" Gideon asked, sure that King Jester must be getting his point by now.

King Jester pondered this question for a moment, his eyes darting from body part to body part as if only by looking at them could he think of them. Finally after mentally and visually touring his Tree Clinger body he silently shook his head from side to side.

"Then why do you think you were given those two gossamer appendages on your back?" Gideon asked.

King Jester answered without hesitation. "Questions, questions. So many questions," He chirped. "Any fool knows that they are our punishment for our original sin. Our Book tells us the first Tree Clinger was brazen enough to think that she and the Creator were one. She did not believe as we do that the Creator is there." King Jester pointed upward. "And we are here. For this original sin of wrong-thinking, that we are more than we appear to be, all future generations of Tree Clingers were to be born with the curse. These grotesque encumbrances on our back are to remind us of our place."

Gideon shook his head in despair. It was a lost cause trying to convince the King to change his mind, but then Kings and all those who held power always had the most to lose by new ideas, by changing the status quo. "Do you mind if we talk with some other Tree Clingers?" he asked.

"Be my guest. Yes, yes. I say be my guest. But you won't change any minds. No indeed. You won't. You won't. We want for nothing, and, even if this curse could allow us to fly, as you say, why would anyone want to fly into the unknown? It is safe here."

"Thank you for your time, King Jester," Gideon said. He was happy to leave, as the pitch of the King's chirp was beginning to make his ears ring.

"No problem. No, no problem at all. Oh, I should warn you and your friend to look out for falling dung. The lower you go the more likely you are to have some fall on you. It is an inevitable part of Tree Clinger life."

It wouldn't be, Gideon thought, if you'd shed your fears and superstitions and learn to fly.

The center section of the tree was the most befouled by Tree Clinger dung, for there was always someone above. The outermost branches were free from soiling, for in the pyramid design of their society no one perched above the outer branches. Being curious and not wanting Tree Clinger dung to fall through his spirit body, Gideon chose to speak to the lucky girl with no perchers above her. He moved to a middle level outer branch and struck up a conversation with the teenage girl, who, had it not been for her bird feet, would have made a great date back on Earth, wings or no wings. It did not pass Gideon's attention that the Tree Clingers had no need for clothes, although umbrellas would have come in handy.

"My, oh my, more visitors," the beautiful young Tree Clinger said. She eyed Gideon admiringly and thought it a pity he had such strange feet, although she was impressed that he was not cursed. Her chirp was softer and had a mellifluous tone to it, more like a dove than a chipmunk.

Gideon introduced himself and Zacharaias. He learned the girl's name was Falola and that she was sixteen-years-old. Of course, the world of the Tree Clingers took only three hundred days to circle its sun, so in Earth time she was only fourteen.

Falola believed the same confining drivel about her wings as did King Jester, but she seemed more curious than the King.

"How do you know about wings and flying?" Falola asked.

"Where I come from the skies are full of flying creatures. We call them birds, and we envied their ability to fly so much that we made machines to take us into the sky. If I had your wings, Falola, I'd be off this dung-covered tree and into the air in a heart beat."

Falola looked up and saw the sun was almost directly overhead. "Oh my, oh my. In just a few minutes my time at the outer edge of my branch will be over. I'm enjoying our talk so much. Would you move in with me? It's not as bad as you might imagine. We Tree Clingers are quite used to it."

"Why do you have to move in? Aren't your places permanently assigned?"

"To a branch, yes," Falola explained. "But there is movement along the branch. Time on the outermost edge, where you find me now, is awarded for meritorious behavior. Curiosity is frowned upon and asking questions is definitely taboo. Since I had gone an entire week without asking a question or being curious about anything I was awarded half a day at the outer position."

"And I assume the middle positions are for offenders of these tabus," Gideon guessed.

"Yes. Unfortunately I spend much of my time there, but the broad leaves are as abundant as the dung. So I never go hungry, and it rains at least once a day. Showering is our greatest pleasure as you may have guessed.

"Sometimes I think I'm defective or must be a direct descendant of the Original Sinner, for I am curious all the time. I

90

ask questions about everything. I don't know how I went a week without asking one, but I really wanted to experience the outer position, just once."

A revolutionary in the making, Gideon thought. He turned to Zack and whispered his plan. Zacharaias agreed, and Gideon turned back to Falola.

"Falola," Gideon began, "you have an opportunity here that may never come your way again. And being the dreamer that you are, you'll regret it the rest of your life if you don't take it."

"Take what, Gideon?" Falola asked, a puzzled look clouding her hazel brown eyes.

"Zack and I want to spread your wings. That's all, just spread your wings. None of your fellow Tree Clingers will do it for you, for their hearts are filled with laws, rules, and fear. I promise you'll not be hurt. You may have to spend some time in the middle for it, but that's nothing you're not used to and, as you said, it rains every day. What do you say?"

All of her life Falola had felt different than the other Tree Clingers. There was something in her that wanted more out of life than eating broad leaves and washing dung from her body, something that longed to know if there was a world outside the Tribal Tree. She was afraid, but her longing overpowered her conditioned judgment.

"Are you sure it won't hurt?" she asked. "No one has ever done this before." Her bird claws began to loosen their grip on the branch.

"One Tree Clinger has. You know the legend," Gideon said.

"You mean the legend of the Tree Clinger that climbed to the top of the tree and disappeared?" Falola asked.

"Yes, but he didn't just vanish into thin air. He spread his

91

wings and discovered the world."

Falola looked around and noticed several Tree Clingers breaking the curiosity taboo. They were looking directly at Gideon, Zack and her. Maybe there are others that think like me, she thought.

Falola took a deep breath. "Okay. Middle of the tree, here I come. Stretch away!"

Gideon and Zacharaias slowly stretched Falola's satin-white wings. Not being fully grown, her wing span fell four feet short of Gideon's twenty-foot estimate. It was enough, however, to catch a gust of wind and lift Falola off her branch.

"Don't be afraid," Gideon said calmly. "Zack and I are right here with you."

"But I am afraid," Falola said. Her body trembled, but her face belied the excitement she felt. Ten Tree Clingers, their curiosity getting the best of them, earned a place in the middle of the tree.

"Move your wings up and down," Gideon instructed the fledgling flier. "Catch the wind and live the life you were meant to live."

Slowly at first, but then with increasing confidence, Falola began to use her wings. Since she had no idea how to maneuver, Gideon and Zack guided her to the top of the tree.

"From here there is nothing in your way, Falola," Zack said. "Learn to use your wings and then return to bring enlightenment to the rest of the Tree Clingers."

"But they'll crucify me if I return. I've violated every rule in our Book."

"It will not be easy, but a life fully lived never is. Many will curse your name, but some will learn from your example and break the bonds of their fear."

Falola hesitated only long enough to say her thanks and to attend to one minor bodily function before spreading her wings once more and soaring into the Land of the Tree Clinger sky. King Jester, for the first time in his life experienced the distinct displeasure of being the recipient of what he had for years rained down upon his fellow Tree Clingers below him.

Chapter Ten

Do you think Falola will return to her Tree Tribe?" Gideon asked as he and Zack thought-traveled leisurely toward the Land of No Opposites.

"She will both return and not return," Zack replied.

"Oh yeah, I forgot. Every possibility gets lived out."

"Each and every moment of your life is a cross-roads, Gideon. At the moment Falola decides to return, another world is ready to accept the possibility not chosen. There is a Gideon McGee alive at this very moment who chose not to risk his life to save his sister, just as there is a Prudence alive at this very moment who listened to the urgent warnings of her brother and stayed off the thin ice of Round Pond."

"I'm not going to remember this, am I?" Gideon asked. A feeling of sadness washed over him.

"Remembering that all of life's possibilities are lived out is not important," Zack said. "What is important is that all possibilities exist at every moment of your life and that your choice at the cross-roads be consciously made, and not be made out of fear."

"The Tree Clingers only had an ice cube worth of the iceberg above the surface, didn't they?" Gideon said, referring to Dr. Spiro's iceberg.

"That's correct, Gideon. Very little of their lives are lived consciously. I chose to show you this version of the Tree Clinger evolution, for it was the most appropriate for your own development. There is a world, however, where the skies are filled with

94

Tree Clingers, who live wherever they choose and whose dung fertilizes their entire planet and not their brothers' and sisters' shoulders."

"Sounds like they have the perfect life," Gideon said, wistfully.

"The perfect life is the creative life, the life fully lived," Zack answered. "Your species has done more to undermine its growth by misunderstanding the meaning of the word 'perfect' than by any other means."

"I don't understand," Gideon said. "There are perfect squares, perfect circles, perfectly straight lines. What is there to understand about perfect? Perfect is perfect."

"There is nothing wrong with applying the word to geometric forms, as you have just done, although extending a geometric form into space causes it to bend, much like a pancake draped over a stick. But that's beside the point I wish to make. The problem arises when you apply the word 'perfect' to the Creator and to yourselves."

"But isn't God perfect?" Gideon asked.

"God is creation itself. When you use the word in this sense it signifies an end state, a completed form. If this were the case, creation would cease to unfold, God would be complete, and the Universe, all Universes, would come to a sudden halt. There is no perfect end-state you are to reach as humans. Creation continues and will never end. Remember, Gideon, you are co-Creators with the Creator. There is no perfect way of living, as you describe it, for it would eliminate all other possibilities.

"Now," Zack continued, "I must prepare you for the world of No Opposites. It is unique in the Universe and, for you, the last schoolroom before you must decide to live in your body or to live out of your body."

95

"What's so special about the world of No Opposites? What's the big deal about opposites?"

"Better you see for yourself than I explain it to you, but in order for us acquire admittance to it we must change our form, for it is a world of only one dimension."

"You mean it's flat like a photographic image?" Gideon asked, surprised at the insight of his question.

"It is like that and more. Are you ready?"

"Ready," Gideon said nervously. He immediately felt his spirit-body changing. Not only did it flatten out like those cartoon characters run over by a steam roller, but his features changed as well. Gideon looked over at Zacharaias, and he was changing in exactly the same way.

"Don't be afraid, Gideon," Zack said, his voice different than before the change. "This is necessary for admittance into the Land of No Opposites."

Gideon noticed that his body was now a carbon copy of Zack's. It was as though they had been cloned from the same cell. Their skin was a pallid grayish-brown, the color one would expect if all colors were mixed together. Then Gideon noticed that every aspect of the body; eyes, teeth, lips, fingernails, everything was this same shade of gray. There were no other colors. It was worse than those old black and white photos he saw when visiting Grandma McGee. At least in those photos there were different shades of white and gray and black. Since both he and Zack were now as flat as a photograph the only way he could discern one bodily feature from another was by the sheen. Each feature had a slightly different brightness to it.

Their bodies were completely hairless, identical in every way, and, strangest of all, were neither male nor female.

"What are we, Zack? I can't tell the difference between you and me. And what is this thing, here?" Gideon pointed to a ribbed, pouch-like area just below his navel.

"That is your reproductive system. The Nopossites, the name for the creatures of this world, do not require a partner to reproduce. They self-fertilize and incubate their young in that pouch. Their children aren't really children since they emerge from the pouch as fully formed adults. The Nopossites don't have a word for children, nor do they have a word for young or old. Nothing ages here. Their lives and bodies are exactly the same from the moment they are born to the moment they die, thirty-five years later."

"Weird, man!" Gideon said. "I'm not sure I want to visit this place."

"But the Land of No Opposites is the land you longed for back on Earth," Zack replied.

"I don't get you. Why would I long for something like this? I'm an 'it' here."

"This is a land of absolute fairness, as you will soon see. Did you not complain on a regular basis that life was not fair. Nopossites' feelings cannot be hurt, for they have no feelings. You will find that their vocabulary is severely limited due to their one-dimensional, completely fair society.

"Our metamorphosis is complete. We may now enter the razor-thin slit, which is the portal to the Land of No Opposites."

Gideon noticed a small rift in the fabric of the Universe much like a letter slot in a door. It was through this small opening that the two entered the Land of No Opposites.

In a one dimensional world only one surface can exist at a time. There was no up or down, front or back, tall or short, fat or skinny. There was nothing that would make one Nopossite stand

97

out in relation to any other Nopossite. The world in which the Nopossites existed was void of color and features, for had there been such things then preferences would have developed and hierarchies established. Without opposites there was never anything the Nopossites had to choose between.

"If all the Nopossites look the same," Gideon said, "how can I tell one from another? How can I tell you from another?"

"The Nopossites have no need to tell one from another, for they have no emotions and are psychologically identical. Don't worry, however. We will not lose each other. I will see to that."

"How can the Nopossites not have emotions?" Gideon asked, puzzled by this most strange and other-worldly place.

"Think for a moment, Gideon." Zack instructed his young charge. "Remember, there are no opposites here. Everything is neutral. Try to describe love to me without using any word that has an opposite. But think of me as a Nopossite, or better yet, here comes one now. Ask it what love is."

There were three Nopossites present on the barren land-scape, Zack, Gideon, and the new arrival, but there was nothing to tell them apart.

"This is my, friend," Gideon said, addressing the Nopossite and pointing to Zack. Before he could continue the Nopossite interrupted.

"Friend?" it asked. "What is this word 'friend?'"

"Friend," Gideon repeated. "You know, someone you like and hang-out with."

"Like? What is this word 'like?'"

"Someone you feel warm toward," Gideon said with increasing frustration.

"You use many words unknown to me," the Nopossite

said. "What is warm?"

"You know, a good feeling."

"What is good?"

Gideon turned to Zack, exasperated.

"There are no opposites here," Zack reminded Gideon. "There's 'friend' whose opposite is 'foe.' Neither friend nor foe can exist here. There's 'like' whose opposite is 'dislike' and therefore neither can be experienced. 'Warm's opposite is 'cool' and the opposite of 'good' is 'bad'. Get it?"

"I get it, but what a pain."

"Pain?" the Nopossite asked. "What is pain?"

"Never mind," Gideon said. "You're driving me crazy."

"What is 'never' and what is 'crazy?'"

Zacharaias began laughing, pleased with himself and enjoying the predicament Gideon was in.

"What is that you are doing?" the Nopossite asked Zack, referring to the laughter it had never seen nor experienced before.

"I would not be able to explain it to you," Zack said. "Do you have a name?"

"We have no names in the Land of No Opposites," it said. "There is no need."

"Why not?" Gideon asked.

"All of our experience is one. My life-experiences are those of everyone else. Addressing one Nopossite is like addressing all Nopossites."

"But surely there must be some differences between you," Gideon said, his annoyance increasing.

"Differences? What are differences?"

Gideon started to explain but thought better of it, realizing that 'different' and 'same' were opposites and therefore could not be experienced by the Nopossites. "Never mind," he said.

"Do you all eat the same food?" Gideon asked.

"Same?"

Gideon rephrased his question. "What do Nopossites eat?"

The Nopossite looked around and pulled a dark gray plant from the flat surface. "This," it said. "We all eat the jalambo plant. It is found everywhere, and we all eat ten of them each day."

"Where do you live? I see no homes. I see nothing, actually."

The Nopossite looked puzzled, as though it was listening to a foreign language. Gideon turned to Zack for help.

"The Nopossites have no word for 'live,' since its opposite is 'die,' and so the two words cannot co-exist. It does not understand 'nothing,' for 'nothing' has its counterpole 'everything.'"

"Forget it," Gideon said, but then remembered 'forget's' opposite is 'remember' and turned away.

"What kind of world is this?" Gideon asked Zack. "There's no life here. These Nopossites are like androids only duller. At least androids have different experiences to relate to. Here, all Nopossites experience life in exactly the same gray manner."

Gideon was visibly upset. Zack just smiled, as this was the effect anticipated when he decided to bring Gideon to the Land of No Opposites. He decided to egg him on further, to stretch his mind as well as his soul.

"I thought you longed for a world of perfect fairness?" Zack asked.

Gideon thought of the Land of What is Good? What is Bad? and of Wu Li. He thought of the Land of the Tree Clingers and Falola and finally of the Gatekeeper.

"Who knows what is fair," Gideon said. "I thought I did, but obviously fairness is not what I was looking for." Gideon grew

100

quiet, his eyes, his mind and his heart surveying this flat one-dimensional world of No Opposites.

"According to Dr. Spiro my dream of the tug-of-war was a big dream. It was about opposites, wasn't it?"

"Was it?" Zacharaias asked.

"It's impossible for us to learn without being in a world of opposites, isn't it? It's impossible for us to feel unless there is something to choose between, right?"

"Go on. Gideon. You're working this one out just fine," Zack said.

"Seeing this Nopossite makes me thankful that we're all different back on Earth. I'd have nothing to choose from. In the Land of No Opposites there would be no Jenny Bloom. As a matter of fact, there would be no need for a Jenny Bloom, for I'd never be struck by Cupid's arrow. I'd have no favorites for there would be nothing to favor. Can Nopossites fall in love?"

"How could they?" Zack replied. "How would one know the experience of love without ever having experienced its absence? How can one learn the healing power of forgiveness if there has never been a wound? How can a heart feel joy, never having experienced sorrow? Can there be a night without a day, a Summer without a Winter? The Good and the Bad is all mixed together, which was well understood by Wu Li. Without this exquisite field of opposites in which you live the entire iceberg would remain underwater. There would be no consciousness, no growth."

"But there is unfairness in the world," Gideon complained. "And some really bad stuff happens. Do we have to experience hatred in order to know what love is?"

"No. As more of your species learns how to truly love one another, hatred will diminish. Hatred is not born out of a void.

101

There is no Original Sin. Where there is no love, hatred will arise. In a deep, mystical sense you are all one, and, as you gradually come to this realization, fewer will be excluded from the circle of love."

"Is both bad and good inside of us when we're born?" Gideon asked.

"No. You are like the Gold center in your dream when you make your entrance into the light and out of the darkness of your mother's womb. At first you perceive nothing as being separate from yourself. The doctor that delivered you, the nurse that assisted her, your mother, your father, all were part of you. You and everything you surveyed were one. All of the energies you were born with had equal voice."

"What do you mean by energies?" Gideon asked.

"You are born with all the potentialities for wholeness. Confidence, creativity, empathy, are all there, as well as what you are most suited to do, be it a carpenter, a priest, an artist, a plumber. As you enter family life, which is determined by your culture, certain energies are encouraged while others are frowned upon. Those energies that are discouraged fall back into the unconscious but remain active. Sometimes, such as in cases of child abuse, the entire real Self falls back into the unconscious, and what the world sees is the false Self."

"I don't get it," Gideon said. "How does the bad get born. Does it come from the false Self?"

"Think about it for a minute," Zack replied. "What if someone took you, threw you in a dark dungeon so you never saw the light of day, bound your arms and legs, and then gagged you?"

"I'd get very angry."

"Then after many years you find a way to loosen your

102

bonds and remove your gag. You move around your dungeon and find a small peep hole, just big enough for you to see out. How would you feel?"

"I'd want out. I'd want to participate in life."

"But how would you feel?"

"Angry," Gideon said. "I'd feel uncontrollable anger."

"What if your jailor forgot he put you down there?" Zack asked. "What would you do?"

"I'd scream, kick the walls, pound on the door. I'd even pee through the peep hole if it would get someone's attention. I'd keep up the noise and disturbance until my jailor remembered I was down in the dungeon."

"Now," Zack said, "what if your dungeon were actually inside your jailor's head and the peep hole was his eyes? Unbeknownst to your jailor, who had forgotten he had put you down there when he was a child, all the anger and disturbance you have been making comes through to him as violence, hatred, and bigotry. Until the jailor hears the cries of the imprisoned true Self his life will not be under his conscious control. Get it?"

"I think so," Gideon answered. "I'm both the jailor and the jailed. But how do I learn to hear the parts of me that I've jailed?"

"By understanding that everything has meaning and that everything that happens is there to move you from your stuck position. The very best way however, is to use other people as a mirror, a reflection of those parts of yourself you've jailed."

"You mean the parts of myself I've buried or refuse to acknowledge I can easily see in other people? How do I know that what I'm seeing is part of my true Self that I've put in the dungeon? Everybody can't be carrying parts of me."

"I thought Jesus said it pretty well," Zack replied. "He said, 'before you pull the mote from your enemy's eye, remove the beam

103

from your own.' What he was saying was that you project onto your enemy what you refuse to see in yourself."

"But it's bad stuff I see in my enemy. Is my true Self bad?" Gideon asked.

"No, it's not bad, it's angry, just as anyone unjustly jailed would be angry. Once you recognize that what you see in your enemy is also in you then a transformation can take place."

"Is it only the bad stuff we project onto others?"

"You're growing wiser by the second, Gideon. Because you have been so conditioned in the West to see yourselves as sinners you refuse to see the good in you. Your heros carry all the good that rightfully belongs to you. You are all heros, a divine spark, only you don't know it yet."

"Let's bring this back to my dream," Gideon said. "The white and black circles represent those parts of me, good and bad, that I've projected onto others, because I refuse to see them in myself. My true Self, the golden circle, tries to draw both projected aspects back into itself and by doing so grows larger. Is that right? Do I become more conscious when I take back what I've projected onto others?"

"Yes, yes, yes!" Zack said, a super nova-sized grin on his face. "If I had a cap and gown I'd dress you for graduation."

"So what happens now?"

"We get out of this restricted world of No Opposites. That's what happens now. You drive."

Chapter Eleven

I 've decided to introduce you to the Incredible Shrinking World," Zack said. "The ISW, as we in the guide business refer to it, may be our most important visit. I saved it until I felt certain about your decision to return to your body, for without your return this lesson would have been wasted. It also comes last on our journey for unless you absorbed the wisdom imparted by your other experiences then the ISW would be meaningless to you."

Gideon felt a sense of pride, not the pride that inflates the ego, but a pride that acknowledges a job well done.

"We will have a guide on this tour," Zack said. "Her name is Sarah and she has endeavored for many years to halt the shrinkage of her planet."

"What's the name of the planet?" Gideon asked.

"The name of this planet is Earth, and on this particular earth the consequences of cause-and-effect are readily apparent to an observer, but not to the inhabitants."

"Where is the planet?"

"There's one in every Universe."

"The Gold Universe has two Earths?" Gideon asked.

"Why not?" Zack replied. "Each Universe has over eighteen billion galaxies. Each galaxy has over one hundred billion stars, and each star has an average of five planets. Do the math. Your universe is no puny thing, just as you are no puny thing."

"How do we get there?"

"Need you ask?" Zack said, arching both white eyebrows. "Just think ISW, right?"

This trip was instantaneous. There were no light shows, no super novas, and no doors to go through. Gideon was becoming an experienced pilot.

Zack and Gideon found themselves on Madison Avenue in New York City standing on the sidewalk in front of the Gleason Building, home of the world's largest advertising firm. Both wore navy-blue pin-stripped three piece suits, button down collars on white linen shirts, gold cuff-links at their wrists and diamond studs in their red power ties.

"Everyone looks overweight," Gideon observed. "And very rich."

He noticed a beautiful woman dressed in a burgundy suit striding purposefully toward Zack and himself. She was decidedly thinner than the other women on the street. Her hair was the color of spun midnight and her teak colored eyes gazed directly into his.

"Hello, Gideon," she said, offering her outstretched hand in greeting. The blackness of her hand stood in stark contrast to Gideon's white. "Zack tells me you're a fast learner. It's too bad I can't say the same for the majority of people on this side of the planet. I'm Sarah."

"What do you mean by this side of the planet?" Gideon asked, forgetting to return Sarah's greeting.

"The west. You know, the developed side, just as on your Earth."

Gideon didn't understand her meaning, but figured it would eventually become clear.

"How have you been Zack?" Sarah asked, turning toward the guide and embracing him in a big bear hug. "It's been several

106

lifetimes."

"Yes it has," Zack replied, returning Sarah's embrace. He noticed Gideon's puzzled look.

"Do you remember the dream you had about the four desert wanderers?" Zack asked.

"The one where they found the city of gold?"

"That's the one. Sarah is like the fourth wanderer to climb the outer wall of the city."

"I woke up," Gideon cut in, "before the fourth wanderer decided whether to follow the others over or climb back down to show the way to those lost in the desert."

"Sarah is one of those that climbed back down," Zack said. "She's one of those soul's whose compassion for others is greater than her individual need of entering the city of gold."

"Is she one of those old souls? You know, one of the fast learners."

"Enough about me, already," Sarah said. "Let's get on with what you came here to get on with."

"Why is everyone so heavy on this planet?" Gideon asked.

"Watch what you say there, young man." Sarah put her hands on her hips and did a pirouette. "Not everyone here is heavy. The heaviest people are right here in New York City, and Madison Avenue in particular."

"I don't get it," Gideon said. "And why is this called the Incredible Shrinking Planet? I don't see anything shrinking. Everyone's big."

"All these big people don't get it either," Sarah replied. "You see, Gideon, New York is the economic center of the world, and Madison Avenue is where the people work who find ways to make people like you and I want things we don't need. They make us feel that our happiness is all wrapped up in the acquisition of things, and they get very rich doing it."

"And fat too, it looks like," Gideon said.

"As the west consumes more than its share of the Earth's bounty, those in the east wither away. Here," Sarah said. "Let me show you."

Sarah placed both hands on Gideon's head. From the right hand he saw a family in the west sitting down to dinner. The table was laden with enough food for ten people eating sensibly, but this was a family of four. There were platters of steaks, mashed potatoes, corn, salads and pies. The four ate to their fill and threw the leftovers into the garbage.

From the left hand Gideon saw another family of four sitting on the dirt floor of a thatched hut. On the floor was enough food for one person eating sparingly. It was divided into four equal shares.

Sarah removed her hands. "What did you see?" She asked.

"Two families eating dinner. One had too much, the other too little."

"Describe the people."

"One family was rich and overweight, the other poor and malnourished."

"I'm going to touch you again," Sarah said. "This time over your heart. I'm going to speed things up dramatically."

The families were similar in age. The parents were in their thirties and the children appeared to be fourteen and five. The family with the abundant life style lived in a suburban community only a few miles from a sprawling shopping mall, whose contents equaled the gross national product of the small impoverished country of the poor family. The needy family lived on a barren plain with only a few scrub bushes in sight.

Gideon saw the family on the right eating and buying, and eating and buying; using and throwing away, using and throwing away. Years passed in a matter of seconds. While the right-hand family was consuming, the left-hand family was searching, searching for fire wood, searching for water, searching for food. While the family on the right was growing fatter, the family on the left grew more and more emaciated. Soon after the scene began, the youngest of the poor family disappeared.

The more the right hand family consumed the more the left hand family suffered. Gideon could not miss the implication.

"Are you showing me that the family on the left doesn't need to starve?" Gideon asked.

"That's exactly what I'm showing you," Sarah answered.

"But what can one family do?" Gideon asked. "It would take the whole world to change to make a difference."

"Evolution is slow," Sarah said. "But it starts with the individual. Change takes place one person at a time. Did you know that it takes sixteen pounds of grain and soybeans, twenty-five hundred gallons of water and the equivalent of one gallon of gasoline to produce one pound of beef? That can feed and warm a whole lot of people.

"Come," Sarah said. "We're going to watch a little TV. But this TV only plays commercials. It's in the Gleason building just behind us."

They passed through the gilded glass doors of the fifty story building and entered an elevator that would take them to the thirteenth floor. They exited into a large waiting room filled with overstuffed chairs and a wall-sized TV screen. In twenty second segments, ad after ad bombarded the room. Gideon noticed that children, in particular, were targeted by the ads and he questioned Sarah about it.

"Children are the most impressionable," Sarah began. "The admen realize that if they can hook one of us early enough they can trick us into believing that what matters most is what we possess. The inner life goes begging. The admen grow consumers. They're gardeners in a sense, but what they grow are the weeds. The weeds choke the flowers.

"The ads tell you to be an individual, but they're making you over in their image."

Gideon watched the TV screen and in twenty second sound and vision bites he began to understand what he did not understand on his home planet. Sarah touched his head as he watched and the TV screen split into halves. On the right was the ad and on the left the effect the ad had on the planet if everyone bought what it was trying to sell. As he watched, Gideon understood why this was the Incredible Shrinking Planet.

This was a throw-away planet. What they took out of the planet to manufacture their products and create their money was never replaced. They saw money as their capital. Natural resources that made everything possible was expendable. As the ads whisked by in rapid succession on the right, representing the use of rain forest lumber, fossil fuels, ore of all sorts, water, and top soil, the planet on the left shrunk perceptibly.

The entire screen changed as Sarah placed her other hand on Gideon's head. He saw beef cattle grazing on the right and for each one an acre of grain disappeared on the left. As a boy his age wiped his hands on a throw-away paper towel, an old-growth tree from the temperate forests disappeared. As a young boy tried on a new pair of high-tech basketball shoes on the right, landfills rose to the height of mountains on the left. These scenes were repeated over and over until Gideon could stand no more. He brushed

110

Sarah's hands away and the screen returned to its normal mode.

As he was about to speak, in walked the largest man he had ever seen. He was dressed like Gideon and Zack, but with ten times the material. Gideon figured it took five acres of cotton to clothe this one ponderous man. He could feel the floor tremble as the man lumbered over to them.

"Well, Sarah," the big man said. "I see you're up to no good again. How did you get into my building?" Henry Gleason asked.

"The security guard must have been on a coffee break," Sarah replied, eyeing the five hundred pounds of Henry Gleason. "I see business is good. You must have gained fifty pounds since I saw you last week."

"Fifty-five," Henry Gleason replied in short breaths. "If business keeps improving I should reach seven hundred by spring. Only the CEO of Macrohard will weigh more. Who are your two skinny friends?"

"They're just visiting," Sarah replied.

Henry Gleason looked at Gideon. He knew his age made him a better prospect than Zack. "Can I interest you in anything?" He asked. "A new TV perhaps? You can never have too many TV's."

Gleason knew the way to one's soul was through TV.

"I already have one, thanks," Gideon answered.

"Well, then, how about a bigger one. Bigger is better. Maybe a new bike. One for the roads, one for the mountains, one for racing, one for loafing, one for downhill, one for uphill, one for going right, one for going left. Or, perhaps a car. You can drive here at twelve. We changed the law to increase sales. You can buy one for going short distances, one for long distances, one for on-road, one for off-road, one for snow, one for rain, one for heat, one

111

for cold. We have front wheel drive, rear wheel drive, two wheel drive, four wheel drive and all wheel drive."

"I can't drive until I'm sixteen," Gideon said. "And I think I'll just borrow my parent's car."

Henry Gleason gasped. "Borrow, not Buy? Sinful. Just sinful. How about some new shoes? My company has done wonders for the shoe business. Why, I remember the days when people actually had to get by with one pair of shoes, and, can you believe it, they lasted for years. Bad for business, that. Now we have shoes for walking, sitting, jumping, and skipping; shoes for grass, sand, rocks, roads, dirt, and ice; shoes for rain, snow, sleet, and shoes for cold and shoes for heat. What will it be? Perhaps one of each? That would be best."

Gideon thought of the five pair of foot wear in his closet at home and felt a twinge of guilt. "I have enough, thanks," he said and ducked as one of Henry Gleason's buttons popped off his vest and whistled past his ear like a bullet.

"I must be able to tempt you with something?" Henry Gleason said, his frustration increasing. "I know. How about some CD's. We have CD's for every kind of taste and all sorts of machines to play them on. We have walk-man, jump-man, run-man, and jog-man. We have sit-man, stand-man, sleep-man and doze-man. You name it. We have it. And the best part is that you just throw them away when your tastes change. We discourage trading."

"Don't you have radio?" Gideon asked.

"We haven't had radio for fifty years," Henry Gleason said proudly. "My father was responsible for that. He figured it cut down on all kinds of sales. The advertising wasn't so great on radio anyway. Dad discovered we could sell more for our clients if we got rid of radio altogether. My father gained two hundred and thirty-three pounds from that discovery. Now, instead of the music industry getting free advertising every time a radio station played their music, they pay us to advertise and nobody gets their product for free. Great idea, huh, kid?"

"How do people who can't afford a CD player get to hear music?" Gideon asked.

"Not my problem, kiddo. Not my problem. My grandfather always said, 'money talks, bullshit walks.' Good man my Grandad. Died at four hundred and eighty-three and three quarter pounds. Started this company, he did.

"Look, it's obvious you're not here to buy or to enlist Gleason's help in selling a product. I don't want any potential customers seeing skinny people like you hanging around. Sarah," Henry Gleason barked. "Get yourself and your light-weight friends out of my building before I call security."

"My pleasure, Henry," Sarah said. "We got what we came for. You better sit down. You're sweating all over your new suit."

"Plenty more where this came from," Henry Gleason replied. "Why, I have suits for hot, suits for cold, suits for driving, suits for flying, suits for high humidity, suits for low humidity..."

Sarah, Zack and Gideon didn't wait for Henry Gleason to finish. They had seen and heard enough. Gideon, was first out of the Gleason Building door and gulped-in the air. He had a sense of suffocating while inside.

"How can you stand it here, Sarah?" Gideon asked. He loosened his tie and threw the diamond tie-tack into the street. A smartly dressed gentleman dove into the gutter after it and as he grabbed the diamond the button on his waist band popped off.

"Is it much different here than on your Earth?" Sarah replied. "It's all a matter of degree."

113

"I don't think I'll ever buy another thing when I get back," Gideon swore.

"You will," Sarah replied. "But with more awareness of the impact your purchase has on the rest of the planet."

"I don't think I need to go east," Gideon said. "The point was well enough made right here in the west."

"It's up to you, Gideon," Sarah said. "You know, I think you're going to climb back down the outer wall of the city of Gold."

"It's not going to be easy, my going back. Is it?"

"There's much yet to learn, Gideon," Zack said. "And you'll learn it on your Earth. It won't be easy, for you have planned a big life for yourself. We staged the Round Pond episode to jump-start you."

"What do you mean, 'we'," Gideon asked.

"That's another story for another time. Are you ready to go back?"

"More ready than ever before. Let's go."

In the flash of a thought Gideon and Zacharaias were back in Norwich, Connecticut, hovering above the hole in the ice of Round Pond.

Chapter Twelve

J erry Denbow had been a fire fighter for ten years and during that time had rescued cats, dogs, birds, one iguana, and many people, but never under such cold conditions. His rescues were performed in the hottest of environments, burning homes, buildings, and barns. Jerry was small for a fireman. At twenty-nine his sixty-six inches and one hundred forty pounds made him the ideal fireman for many tight situations that a larger man would find impossible. Pound for pound Jerry was the strongest man on the ten-station Norwich Fire Department.

It took Prudence thirty-six seconds to sprint the hundred yards to the fire station and another twenty to relate Gideon's dire predicament. She could have cut the telling of the story to fifteen seconds had she not been shivering so badly. There were no EMTs available, as they were out on an emergency. The call was placed for an EMT vehicle while Jerry and two other firemen gathered ropes, emergency medical equipment, and blankets. Prudence's wet clothes were removed and she was wrapped in two woolen blankets as the fire fighters prepared.

Jerry Denbow tied one end of the rope around his waist and held the other in his left hand as he raced toward Round Pond. Jerry was the first to reach the frozen pond. John Harris and Tim Stein, both twenty-year firemen and both a head taller and sixty pounds heavier than Jerry, reached the pond a moment later. They stood on the bank holding the ropes as Jerry Denbow inched his way like a snake toward the hole in the ice.

Two minutes had passed since Prudence burst through the fire house doors, and Jerry was well aware of how long the brain could go without oxygen. Four minutes was the usual limit before irreparable brain damage occurred. Jerry was hopeful that the near-freezing temperature of the Round Pond water would give him some extra time. He knew of cases where children survived and lived normal lives after being submerged in icy waters for over an hour.

"I can see a light under that fireman on the ice," Gideon said, as he and Zack hovered above the scene. "What is it?"

"It's his guide supporting the ice from below so Jerry doesn't fall through," Zack said. "He's borrowing energy from many other guides to accomplish this."

Not knowing that there was help from a source he could neither see nor feel, Jerry moved cautiously along the ice. As Gideon had done before him he was on his belly, thus dispersing his weight over a larger area. He was sacrificing time for safety, for he knew if he fell through the ice before reaching Gideon's hole, all might be lost. John Harris and Tim Stein provided just enough slack in the two ropes to pull Jerry back should he begin to break through, yet not hinder him in his forward progress.

It was a weird feeling Gideon had as he watched Jerry, only two or three feet from the break in the ice, prepare to enter the stinging waters of Round Pond.

"He doesn't even know me," Gideon said to his companion. "Why is he risking his life for me? It has to be more than just his job that makes him put his own life in peril."

"It is, Gideon. It is called love. At the core of our being we are all One, and it is at times of crisis such as this that this realization breaks through. Not on a conscious level, but it is the

116

engine that is driving Jerry toward you. He doesn't realize that in the grander scheme of life he is saving a part of himself by saving you."

"He's very brave," Gideon said.

Zacharaias looked at Gideon, proud of the changes their journey had wrought.

Jerry reached the edge of the hole and peered down. "I can't see a thing," he yelled back to his partners. "Give me some slack. I'm going in."

The iciness of the water was like a jolt of electricity coursing through his body. It was so cold it burned. Jerry understood he'd have to find the body on the first or second dive, for his body would be too numb to attempt a third. As he headed to the murky bottom he prayed.

Gideon and Zack descended into the water to observe. Jerry felt along the muddy bottom, for he was able to keep his eyes open for no more than a few seconds at a time. The frigid water felt like daggers stabbing each eye.

"I'm to your left, Jerry. Just three feet," Gideon yelled, feeling useless in this situation. He knew the fireman couldn't hear him.

Jerry opened his eyes, hoping against hope to see Gideon's body in the darkness. The pain was excruciating, and he was running out of air. He had to surface. Jerry tugged on his rope, and John and Tim hauled him up. He gasped as his head broke the surface.

"I can't see anything down there," he yelled through rapidly numbing lips. "I'm good for one more try. If I find him, haul us up fast. I'll tug on the rope."

Jerry took a deep breath and headed into the depths one last time. The cold was rapidly robbing him of his coordination, and he knew he would have to practically land on top of Gideon if he were to save him.

"Can't his guide help him?" Gideon asked Zack, realizing that his choice of returning to his body was soon to be taken from him.

"No. He's using all his energy and some of his fellow guides to support the ice." Zacharaias turned and looked directly into Gideon's eyes. "You've decided to live out your life."

"Yes. I want to go back. Can't you do anything to help Jerry?"

"To do so I'll need to leave you. You won't see me again in this form, but know that I love you and will be with you until it is your choice to leave your body behind."

Gideon understood. "I love you Zack, and in some way I'll always remember your kindness and gentle understanding. Go! Help Jerry."

Zacharaias embraced his young friend then turned his attention back to Jerry Denbow. He was two feet from the bottom and about ready to open his eyes. Zack was prepared. The instant Jerry Denbow raised his protective eyelids Zacharaias shot into Gideon's body himself and infused it with a burst of light that drew the hero's attention.

Jerry moved instantly to where he had seen the odd flash of light and reached out his hand. He felt Gideon's lifeless body, but was too numb and too disoriented to think much about the light he saw. Time was running out. He grabbed the body with one arm and yanked on the rope with the other then tightly wrapped both arms around Gideon's waist.

John Harris and Tim Stein knew from the pull of the rope that Jerry had Gideon's body in tow. They heard the snapping of

118

twigs behind them and knew the EMTs had arrived. They didn't know that Prudence, refusing to leave, insisted on going back to the pond with them. Jerry Denbow's head was the first to break the surface. With the last of his remaining strength he heaved Gideon onto the ice and secured the second rope around his body while he stayed in the water. Jerry knew the ice wouldn't support both of them.

Within seconds Gideon was on dry land and the EMTs began their work. Tim and John hauled their partner to safety and tended to his needs while the Medical Technicians busied themselves with Gideon's lifeless body. Gideon's spirit hovered above the scene, mesmerized by all the activity and not sure what to do to get back into his body.

"I got no pulse, no respiration," Sally Tweedle yelled at her partner while simultaneously beginning chest compressions. Harry Bogue cleared Gideon's airway, inserted the mouthpiece of the respirator, and began squeezing the black air bag.

"You better not die, Gideon McGee," Prudence screamed through her sobs. "I'll hate you forever if you die."

Gideon had not felt greater love for his sister than at that moment. How could he not have seen how much she loved him before? He began to feel a strange tugging sensation at the point where the silver thread was attached to the back of his head.

Sally Tweedle stopped her chest compressions long enough to bend over and place her ear on Gideon's chest. Hearing no heartbeat she turned and grabbed two chest paddles connected to a high-voltage generator. She quickly placed conducting-gel on each paddle, situated them on each side of Gideon's chest, and yelled "clear." Harry Bogue stood back. Prudence held her breath. As the electrical charge surged through his body, jump starting his heart, Gideon was sucked back into his physical self, and everything went black.

"I've got a heartbeat," Sally yelled. "It's weak, but I got one. Harry, start an I.V.. We've got to get him to the hospital fast. His body temperature is 64 degrees. We've got to get it up."

They moved Gideon to a stretcher, covered him with blankets, and carried him quickly through the woods to the idling EMT truck. Prudence, still wrapped in a blanket and shivering badly, joined her brother in the truck. A call had been placed to Clara McGee, and she and Rupert were already on their way to Backus Hospital, three miles away.

While Harry Bogue drove, Sally attached the heart monitor. Twenty-four beats per minute, compared to his normal seventy-five, was dangerously low and was a result of his extremely low body temperature. The cold water that caused the low body temperature was both bad and good. It was bad in that such a low body temperature is life threatening, but good in that it may have preserved brain function during the period Gideon's heart stopped.

"Is Gideon going to be alright?" Prudence asked through chattering teeth.

"I don't know, Honey," Sally said. "The doctors will do all they can, but right now only the good Lord knows the answer to your question."

"He's just got to be alright. He saved my life. God couldn't take him after he did such a good thing."

"Life just doesn't seem fair sometimes, does it, honey?" Sally called all children, Honey.

Prudence shrugged her shoulders and sobbed the rest of the way to the hospital. She felt great sadness at the possibility of Gideon's death and unbearable guilt that she was responsible. Why didn't she heed Gideon's warning, she thought. Prudence prayed silently through her tears and her shivering.

An emergency medical team awaited the arrival of the EMT truck and its cargo. Dr. Betty Dow had dealt with many drowning victims during her twenty-five years of Emergency Room practice. She was a tall, thin woman with streaks of gray splashed throughout her short brown hair. Dr. Dow didn't believe in Clairol. She thrived on the excitement and tension of the emergency room and ran five miles a day to keep in shape for its demands. Dr. Dow spoke to Gideon's parents, who arrived a few minutes earlier, but was unable to give them any information regarding his condition or that of Prudence.

"We're here, Honey," Sally Tweedle said through the backing-up warning signal of her truck. "Dr. Dow is the best around and if Gideon can be fixed, she's the one to do it."

"My parents are going to kill me," Prudence said, almost wishing they would.

Sally smiled. "I think they're going to be so happy to see you're okay that scolding you for playing on thin ice will be the furthest thing from their mind."

"Maybe," Prudence whimpered.

"Now give your brother a kiss. You might not see him again for a while. Dr. Dow is going to be very busy with him."

Prudence did as she was directed, then Sally laid her down on the second stretcher. The back doors of the truck opened, and two men slid Gideon out and rushed him into the Emergency Room's number one examining room. As Dr. Dow directed the placement of the electrodes to monitor heart and brain activity, Prudence's parents greeted her entrance into the number two examining room.

"I'm sorry, Mom," Prudence cried. "I didn't know the ice

was thin. I didn't believe Gideon when he warned me. I thought he was just being a jerk. It's all my fault."

Prudence was sobbing hysterically by the time she finished her confession. Mrs. McGee hugged her tightly and rocked her gently. "There, there, Pru," she said. "It's not your fault. I love you."

Clara McGee kissed her daughter tenderly on her forehead and wiped the tears from her eyes with the warm skin of her fingers then did the same to herself.

"How do you feel, Sweetie?" Mr. McGee asked his daughter. His arms were tightly wrapped around both his daughter and his wife.

"I feel okay, Daddy," Prudence said. "I'm just cold."

"Can you tell your mother and I what happened?"

As Prudence told the story Dr. Dow grew hopeful that Gideon would recover. His heart rate was increasing steadily, and was up to fifty beats per minute. His body temperature was also rising. Although her face didn't show it, Dr. Dow was concerned over the electroencephalogram reading. Gideon's brain activity was increasing, but still depressed. She could not be sure there wouldn't be permanent brain damage should Gideon recover. The chances he would suffer from speech and motor impairment was high. Dr. Dow kept her suspicions to herself for the moment.

After doing all she could for him in the Emergency Room Dr. Dow transferred Gideon to intensive care then walked the short distance to examining room number two and informed the three McGees of Gideon's condition.

"You mean Gideon won't be able to talk?" Prudence cried.

"I'm not saying that, Prudence," Dr. Dow said. She knew what happened on the Round Pond ice and understood how badly

Prudence felt. "Your brother's speech might be just as it always was, I don't know. But in cases like this there is always a chance of speech being affected."

Dr. Dow turned to Clara and Rupert McGee. "All of Gideon's vital signs are improving. The chances are fair to good that he will pull through with all functions intact. I told you of the speech and motor problems since there is some potential for impairment. I've called in Dr. Archer for a neurological consult. He'll be here shortly."

Prudence was admitted to the pediatrics ward for observation while Gideon's spirit struggled to gain control over its body. It would be another ten days before he came out of his coma, and although no one noticed, Zacharaias sat by his side the entire time.

Chapter Thirteen

Ten days had passed from the time Gideon first saw Zacharaias appear in the waters of Round Pond to his first conscious moment. His eyes opened slowly to a darkened room. The curtains, green and thick, were drawn to block the morning sun, as though sunlight was something to be avoided at all costs. As consciousness gradually returned so did his memory of Zacharaias.

"Was it all just a dream?" he asked to an empty room. Simon and Prudence were in school, his father had to return to work, and his mother just stepped out for coffee. "Zack! Are you here?"

Gideon looked about the room and noticed his mother's coat on a chair by his bed. The knowledge that his mother was nearby eased some of his anxiety, but he needed to know, he needed a sign, that his experiences after falling through the ice were real. He heard someone enter the room and turned to the sound. In walked an older man, Gideon guessed to be fifty, maybe fifty-five years old. His hair was originally jet black, but the years and hard times had streaked it with white, the color of his hospital orderly uniform. He wore a hearing aid over his left ear that was whistling like a tea kettle, but he seemed not to notice.

The man with the whistling ear walked to the side of Gideon's bed, stooped over and retrieved the waste-basket that was filled with his mother's Styrofoam coffee cups.

"Someone drinks a lot of coffee," the orderly said, turning his face to Gideon.

124

"Must be my mother," Gideon said, groggily.

"What's that?" the orderly asked. "Sounded like you said 'musky high brother.'" He fiddled with his hearing aid, and the whistling stopped. "This damn hearin' aid's twelve years old. Supposed to last only five. Can't afford a new one, though. Seems only the well-off can afford to hear. Says somethin', don't it?"

Gideon looked at the orderly and noticed the black name tag over his left shirt-pocket.

"How long have you been working here, Zack?" Gideon asked, knowing he had received the sign he asked for.

"Started this mornin'," Zack replied. "Strangest darn thing. I been hopin' to get this job, good benefits an' all, but they hired someone else just yesterday. This A.M. they call me and say this other fella' decided not to take the job and they up an' asked me to come right in. Darndest thing." Zack reached up and scratched his head as though the scratching would make things more clear to him.

"I like your name," Gideon said.

Zack looked at him and smiled. Gideon thought he saw him wink, but couldn't be sure as his brain was still in a fog bank. "Zacharaias is an old biblical name. Been in my family for generations. I'm named after my great grandfather Zacharaias Moebius. He was a guide for wagon trains headin' west to settle the new frontier."

"He was a guide?" Gideon asked.

"Best there ever was. Not famous, mind you. Just the best."

"I bet he was," Gideon agreed. "How did you lose your hearing?"

"Vietnam. Got a little too close to a frag-grenade. Blew out both eardrums and left me with nerve deafness. Also left my right leg as fertilizer for the Nam countryside. Bad experience, but

125

taught me a lot."

"What did it teach you?"

"You wouldn't understand," Zack said. "Too young." He emptied the waste basket into the larger trash can on wheels he left just outside the door.

"Try me. Maybe I'll surprise you," Gideon said before Zack could move on to the next room.

"Maybe." Zack walked back into Gideon's room and stood by his bed. "When I lost my hearin' and my leg, they was replaced by an anger so deep I get dizzy thinkin' about it. I cursed God. I cursed life for being so unfair. I wasn't a person you wanted to be around. No sir. But that was then. When I look back on it now I thank God for takin' my ears and my leg."

"Why is that?" Gideon asked.

"I would never have met my wife. She was a nurse in the V.A. hospital where I healed-up, so to speak. We had the two best kids a father could ever want."

"Who knows what's good and what's bad?" Gideon asked.

"What's that?" Zack adjusted the volume of his hearing aid.

"Nothing."

Zack shrugged his shoulders, smiled at Gideon and limped out of his room.

"Nice boy you got there, ma'am," Zack said as Gideon's mother brushed past him as he left the room.

Clara McGee turned to the nurse's station, tears in her eyes. "Nurse! Nurse!" she yelled. "He's awake. Gideon came out of his coma."

* * *

Despite the tests run over the next several days, Gideon

knew he would recover. He also knew that his life had changed irrevocably. In between the blood tests, the heart tests, and the brain tests Gideon spent his time visiting the other kids in the pediatric ward. He was drawn by a force he could not explain into the rooms of the sick children. Room 113 had a particularly strong pull, and it lured him to its doorway. Gideon noticed the name-plate on the outside wall next to the door, and his heart began to race. He entered the dimly lit room and had an overpowering urge to draw open the curtains. Since his experience with Zacharaias, Gideon had found a new appreciation of sunlight. He couldn't explain it. He only knew it made him feel better.

The young girl sitting up in her hospital bed couldn't have been more than ten years old, yet her eyes shined with the brightness Gideon recalled seeing in the Gatekeeper's. She had no hair and held a golden brown teddy bear to her chest. Tarla Zondata's face broke into a wide smile as she noticed Gideon in her doorway. Gideon remembered Tarla and her spirit guide, Zondata, from his trip to the Diamond Universe and knew this girl's name was more than mere coincidence. He walked to her curtain and let the sun fill the room.

With the sun at his back he asked Tarla if she recognized him.

"No," she said, smiling. "But you look like an angel. Are you here to take me to heaven?"

Gideon looked behind him and realized the sun's glare in the suddenly-brightened room must have given Tarla the impression that he had a halo surrounding his body.

"It's the sun," he said and moved to the other side of Tarla's bed that was littered with stuffed animals. He moved aside a fuzzy giraffe and sat down.

"I just woke up and thought you were my guardian angel,"

she said, as though what she was saying was as common as saying hello.

"No," Gideon replied. "I'm just an ordinary kid."

"My mother says there are no ordinary kids. She says we're all special, but by the time we grow up we all forget. Why did you ask if I knew you?"

"I met someone like you in a place far away. For a moment I thought you were her. You have leukemia, don't you?"

"Yes," Tarla said. "How did you know?"

"A lucky guess. Has your brother been treating you kindly?"

Tarla lightly slapped her cheek while her jaw opened wide in amazement. "Ron told you about me, didn't he?"

Gideon smiled, content in allowing Tarla her belief that it was her brother who had informed him about her condition.

"You're going to get better, Tarla, and I have a suspicion that Ron isn't going to be mean to you anymore. I think your illness may have been a great gift to him."

Tarla reached out and took Gideon's hand in hers. "Why are you in the hospital?" she asked. "Do you have leukemia, too?"

Gideon moved his thumb tenderly over the frail fingers of Tarla Zondata. "I died for a little while, and the doctors are just keeping an eye on me."

"How does someone die for a little while?" Tarla asked.

"I can't explain it. At least not yet anyway, but I feel like I left a part of me behind. You see, Tarla, I was a lot like your brother. The part of me that was like Ron is what died. I feel very different."

"I feel different than before I got sick, too," Tarla said. "I can't explain it, but it's true. It's like I feel more grown up."

Gideon bent over and kissed the young girl on her forehead then walked to the door. He turned and said good-bye. As he headed out her door he heard Tarla's voice.

"I saw the light on you before you opened the curtains."

He hesitated long enough to acknowledge her comment then left.

Gideon felt strangely peaceful, as though a great burden had been lifted from his shoulders. As he walked back to his room he thought about what that burden might be. Before his dream, as he decided to call his experience, he had been taught that science reigned supreme, that his mind was a result of the random firing of billions of neurons in his brain, that life itself was the result of an infinite number of cosmic coincidences and was therefore no more meaningful than a frog being flattened by the tire of a speeding truck. He was taught that accidental death was meaningless and that life itself had no significance. Nobody ever told him that everything is connected. Nobody told him that death was not to be feared. As he entered his room and saw Jenny Bloom sitting in the chair next to his bed, he knew what burden had been lifted. It was the burden of believing that life was unfair, that there could be bad without the good. It was the burden of living life as though it had no meaning.

Jenny Bloom turned as she heard Gideon enter the room. She had been lost in the thoughts of her latest interview with Dr. Spiro that last took place while Gideon was in a coma.

"You seem different," Jenny said softly.

Gideon sat on the edge of his bed. "I feel different," he said. "You look great. How have you been?"

"I can't believe you're asking about me when you're the one that died. Everyone at school is talking about it. Even Dr. Spiro is curious. He'd like to see you when you get out of the hospital."

Gideon wanted to tell her the whole story, but something held him back. It wasn't the right time, nor the right place.

"You saw Dr. Spiro again?" Gideon asked.

"Yes," Jenny replied. "I had to finish our project on dreams. It was due yesterday and I put your name on it next to mine. Dr. Spiro talked about that dream you had. The one about the tug of war. Do you remember?"

"Sure. What did he say?" Gideon remembered the Gate-keeper and how he began interpreting the tug-of-war dream before being interrupted. The same thing happened during the first meeting with Dr. Spiro. He wondered if he wasn't ready to hear what had to be said.

"He said all of us have a center. A Self he called it, and that your dream could have been the dream of any of us. It was about this higher Self."

Gideon nodded. A knowing look spread across his face.

Jenny continued. "The black and white halves of the first circle, the one that split apart, represents the opposites that are in all of us. He even said there's an inner man and woman in us all. Can you believe it?"

Gideon took Jenny's hand in his.

"Anyway, Dr. Spiro said that we're always expressing one half of the opposites while the other is repressed. We uncon-sciously keep the repressed part at bay, which he says represents the splitting apart of the black and white circle. The higher Self is the gold circle that appears and tries to draw the black and white halves back to itself. He said that the real Self, the gold circle, can only grow when the opposites are brought together in a conscious way, and it will try anything to bring them together. In your case he thinks this dream means really big things for you if you can

130

unite the opposites. To be honest though, I'm not sure what it all means."

"Maybe I'll be able to explain it to you some day," he said.

Gideon thought of the Land of No Opposites and understood that life on Earth had to be the way it was. He remembered how dull and emotionless seemed the Nopposite he and Zack spoke to.

Jenny glanced at her watch. "I have to be going, Gideon," she said. "My mother wants me home by four. Since her accident she doesn't want me driving after dark."

"Thanks for coming," Gideon said. "It means a lot to me to have you here."

Jenny stood up and kissed Gideon lightly on the lips. As she walked out of the room Gideon thought how lucky he was and then caught the thought. It wasn't luck at all. It wasn't a coincidence that Jenny was there and it wasn't a coincidence that she related to him differently than before. He was now a different Gideon McGee, one that drew people to him. A part of the old Gideon remained at the bottom of Round Pond, just as a part of Ron Zondata died with Tarlas' leukemia, and just as part of Falola died as she spread her wings and flew for the first time in the Land of the Tree Clingers.

Gideon turned toward his window and noticed that dusk was upon the face of the earth. No longer was he afraid to sleep. No longer was he afraid of living. Gideon McGee had died. Long live Gideon McGee.

EPILOGUE

Gideon McGee was never the same after his experience at the bottom of Round Pond. The doctors and scientists never checked on whether his view of the world had been altered. They investigated vision, memory, hearing, coordination, muscle tone, and strength, but never thought to check on what really changed during his five minutes under the waters of Round Pond. Even if they had thought of it, how does one measure the growth of one's soul?

"You seem different," people who knew him would say, just as Jenny had. Maybe it was his hair that now captured and reflected the light of the sun. Maybe it was his body that seemed taller and stood more erect. Gone was the slouch that Gideon used to carry about. More than anything else however, it was Gideon's eyes. They seemed older, but with a light that was not dependent upon the sun. Some said he smiled more since his accident. Other's said he was more confident and maybe it was all these things.

Gideon knew what was different and promised that someday he would find a way to tell the world that they, too, are so much more than they think they are. In the meantime he went on living, knowing that he would experience the bad as well as the good, knowing that behind all the appearances, behind everything that seemed so real, a universe of other realities awaited. But the one that was most important, the one that mattered most, was the one he was in at this very moment.

The End

132

ORDER FORM

Please send_____ copies of *Gideon McGee's Dream* to the following address:

Name:_____

Address:_____

City:_____**State:**_____**Zip:**_____

Sales tax: Please add 6% for books shipped to Connecticut addresses.($.66/book)

Number of Copies X $10.95_____

Shipping & Handling:$2.75 1st copy
$1.75 ea. add. Copy_____
Sales Tax for CT Residents_____

Total:_____

Make check out to Zacharaias Press and mail to: Zacharaias Press
P.O. Box 163
86 Sunnyside St.
Yantic, CT 06389